Samuel French Acting Edition

Shakespeare in Love

Based on the screenplay by
Marc Norman & Tom Stoppard

Adapted for the stage by
Lee Hall

Music by
Paddy Cunneen

Originally produced on the West End by Disney Theatrical
Productions & Sonia Friedman Productions, directed by Declan
Donnellan, and designed by Nick Ormerod

be invented, including mechanical, electronic, photocopying, recording, videotaping, or otherwise, without the prior written permission of the publisher. No one shall upload this title(s), or part of this title(s), to any social media websites.

For all enquiries regarding motion picture, television, and other media rights, please contact Concord Theatricals Corp.

MUSIC USE NOTE

Licensees are solely responsible for obtaining formal written permission from copyright owners to use copyrighted music in the performance of this play and are strongly cautioned to do so. If no such permission is obtained by the licensee, then the licensee must use only original music that the licensee owns and controls. Licensees are solely responsible and liable for all music clearances and shall indemnify the copyright owners of the play(s) and their licensing agent, Concord Theatricals Corp., against any costs, expenses, losses and liabilities arising from the use of music by licensees. Please contact the appropriate music licensing authority in your territory for the rights to any incidental music.

IMPORTANT BILLING AND CREDIT REQUIREMENTS

If you have obtained performance rights to this title, please refer to your licensing agreement for important billing and credit requirements.

SHAKESPEARE IN LOVE was first presented at the Noël Coward Theatre, London, produced by Disney Theatrical Productions and Sonia Friedman Productions, on July 22, 2014. The production was directed by Declan Donnellan, with music by Paddy Cunneen, choreography by Jane Gibson, scenic design by Nick Ormerod, lighting design by Neil Austin, sound design by Simon Baker, fight direction by Terry King, casting by Siobhan Bracke CDG, and associate direction by Oli Rose. The cast of twenty-eight, in alphabetical order, was as follows:

TILNEY	Ian Bartholomew
WILL SHAKESPEARE	Tom Bateman
RALPH	Tony Bell
KATE	Daisy Boulton
VIOLA DE LESSEPS	Lucy Briggs-Owen
QUEEN ELIZABETH	Anna Carteret
ENSEMBLE	Michael Chadwick
HENSLOWE	Paul Chahidi
ENSEMBLE	Tom Clegg
ENSEMBLE	Ryan Donaldson
ROBIN / FREES / MUSICAL DIRECTOR	Tim van Eyken
MOLLY / MISTRESS QUICKLY	Janet Fullerlove
BURBAGE	David Ganly
SIR ROBERT DE LESSEPS	Richard Howard
SAM / FIGHT CAPTAIN	Harry Jardine
ENSEMBLE	Amy Merchant
NURSE	Abigail McKern
PETER / BARMAN	Sandy Murray
MARLOWE	David Oakes
WABASH	Patrick Osborne
ENSEMBLE	Timothy O'Hara
ADAM / BOATMAN / MUSICIAN	Thomas Padden
WESSEX	Alistair Petrie
NED ALLEYN	Doug Rao
LAMBERT / GUARD / MUSICIAN	Elliott Rennie
FENNYMAN	Ferdy Roberts
WEBSTER	Colin Ryan
NOL / MUSICIAN	Charlie Tighe

SHAKESPEARE IN LOVE made its North American debut at the Stratford Festival in Stratford, Ontario on April 29, 2016. The cast of twenty-one was as follows:

SAM . . . . Thomas Mitchell Barnet

NED ALLEYN . . . . .Brad Hodder

WILL SHAKESPEARE . . . . Luke Humphrey

PETER / VALENTINE. . . . . .Josh Johnston

KATE / MISTRESS QUICKLY / DANCE CAPTAIN . . . . Ruby Joy

FENNYMAN. . . . . Tom McCamus

FREES / ROBIN / MUSICIAN . . . . George Meanwell

ADAM / BOATMAN . . . . Mike Nadajewski

QUEEN ELIZABETH / MOLLY . . . . Sarah Orenstein

HENSLOWE . . . . Stephen Ouimette

LAMBERT / NOL / MUSICIAN . . . . .Trevor Patt

RALPH / FIGHT CAPTAIN. . . . . Gareth Potter

WABASH . . . . .Andrew Robinson

NURSE . . . . Karen Robinson

BURBAGE . . . . Steve Ross

WEBSTER . . . . Tal Shulman

CATLING / CONDELL / LADY CAPULET . . . . Colin Simmons

TILNEY / SIR ROBERT DE LESSEPS. . . . . Michael Spencer-Davis

VIOLA DE LESSEPS . . . . Shannon Taylor

MARLOWE . . . . .Saamer Usmani

WESSEX. . . . . Rylan Wilkie

Note: The London production featured four onstage actor-musicians, while the Stratford production featured two. Both productions used a live dog.

Special thanks to Oregon Shakespeare Festival.

CHARACTERS

WILL SHAKESPEARE – poet and playwright
KIT MARLOWE – colleague, friend, and inspiration

FENNYMAN – the money
LAMBERT & **FREES** – Fennyman's henchmen
HENSLOWE – owner and manager of the Rose Theatre

RICHARD BURBAGE – lead actor of the Chamberlain's Men
MISTRESS QUICKLY – wardrobe mistress
Actors playing **VALENTINE** and **PROTEUS**
DOG
Burbage's **HEAVIES** (2)

QUEEN ELIZABETH I
EDMUND TILNEY – the Lord Chamberlain
VIOLA DE LESSEPS – disguises herself as actor **THOMAS KENT**
NURSE – servant to Viola
SIR ROBERT DE LESSEPS – Viola's father
LORD WESSEX – betrothed to Viola
CATLING – guard at De Lesseps Hall
GUARDS (2) at De Lesseps Hall
BOATMAN

WAITER
BARMAN
MOLLY & **KATE** – tavern whores
MUSICIANS

RALPH – novice actor, plays Nurse and Petruchio
NOL – novice actor, plays Benvolio and Samson
ROBIN – novice actor, plays Lady Capulet
ADAM – novice actor, plays Gregory, Benvolio, and Servingman
JOHN WEBSTER – street urchin, aspires to be a player
WABASH – novice actor, Henslowe's stammering tailor

NED ALLEYN – lead actor of the Admiral's Men, plays Mercutio
SAM – actor, plays Juliet
PETER – actor, plays Tybalt
Other actors, including one who plays **ABRAHAM**

SETTING

London

TIME

1593

ACT ONE

Scene One

(Will's room.)

[MUSIC NO. 1: "OPENING – MARLOWE'S THEME"]

*(**WILL** is writing at his desk.)*

WILL. Shall I compare...

Shall I compare...

Shall I compare...the...um...

Shall I compare thee...

Shall I compare thee to a...to a...?

Shall I compare thee to a...sum...a sum...a something, something...

Damn it.

Shall I compare thee to a mummer's play?

Shall I compare thee...to...an autumn morning? An afternoon in springtime? Zounds.

*(**MARLOWE** enters.)*

MARLOWE. A sonnet. I thought you were writing a play.

WILL. A month overdue to Henslowe but nothing comes. I have lost my gift, Kit. I don't know what it is. My quill is broken, my well is dry. The proud tower of the imagination hath collapsed completely.

MARLOWE. Interesting. And how are your marital relations, Will?

WILL. The Hathaways?

MARLOWE. The bedroom.

WILL. As cold as her heart.

MARLOWE. So you are free to love.

WILL. Yet not to write so it seems. Leave me, Kit.

MARLOWE. I've almost finished my new play for Burbage. More blood and thunder but he pays well for it. I hear he plays your *Two Gentlemen of Verona* for Her Majesty this very afternoon.

WILL. My play, for the Queen!

MARLOWE. A summer's day.

WILL. What?

MARLOWE. "A summer's day." Start with something lovely, temperate, and thoroughly trite. Gives you somewhere to go.

(**MARLOWE** *leaves.*)

WILL. *(unconvinced)* A summer's day?!

Shall I compare thee...to a...summer's day? Mmmm? Thou art more...something something something...

Scene Two

(The Rose Theatre.)

[MUSIC NO. 2: "THE HENCHMEN"]

(LAMBERT *and* **FREES** *have* **HENSLOWE** *over hot coals as* **FENNYMAN** *looks on.)*

HENSLOWE. Arrrrgghhh!!!!!

FENNYMAN. You mongrel! Why do you howl when it is I who am bitten? What am I, Mister Lambert?

LAMBERT. Bitten, Mister Fennyman.

FENNYMAN. How badly, Mister Frees?

FREES. Twelve pounds, one shilling, and fourpence, Mister Fennyman, plus interest.

HENSLOWE. I can pay you!

FENNYMAN. When? Mister Henslowe?

HENSLOWE. Two weeks. Three at the most. Aaagh. For pity's sake.

FENNYMAN. Drop him.

HENSLOWE. Aaaaggh!

FENNYMAN. Where will you get...

FREES. Sixteen pounds, five shillings, and ninepence...

HENSLOWE. I have a wonderful new play!

FENNYMAN. A play?

HENSLOWE. A play, Mister Fennyman.

FENNYMAN. Let him have it.

HENSLOWE. Aaaaggh! It's a comedy.

FENNYMAN. Cut off his nose.

HENSLOWE. Aaaaggh! A new comedy.

FENNYMAN. And his ear.

HENSLOWE. By Will Shakespeare.

FENNYMAN. Who?

HENSLOWE. His *Two Gentlemen of Verona* is to be played for the Queen at Whitehall today, acted by Richard Burbage and the Chamberlain's Men.

FENNYMAN. Shakespeare? Never heard of him.

HENSLOWE. I think he has potential. We will be partners, Mister Fennyman.

FENNYMAN. Partners?

HENSLOWE. The play's a crowd tickler – mistaken identities, a shipwreck, a pirate king, a bit with a dog, and love triumphant.

FREES. Didn't you see that one, Lambert?

LAMBERT. Yeah, and I didn't like it.

HENSLOWE. Aaaaggh! But this time it is by Shakespeare.

FENNYMAN. What's it called?

HENSLOWE. *Romeo and Ethel the Pirate's Daughter.*

FENNYMAN. Good title. A play takes time. Find actors… rehearsals, let's say open in three weeks. That's – what – five hundred groundlings at tuppence each, in addition four hundred backsides at three pence – a penny extra for a cushion, call it two hundred cushions, say two performances for safety. How much is that, Mister Frees?

FREES. Twenty pounds to the penny.

FENNYMAN. Correct!

HENSLOWE. But I have to pay the actors and the author.

FENNYMAN. A share of the profits.

HENSLOWE. There's never any profits.

FENNYMAN. Of course not!

HENSLOWE. Mister Fennyman, I think you may have hit on something.

FENNYMAN. Sign here.

HENSLOWE. It's blank.

FENNYMAN. I know.

Scene Three

(Whitehall Palace, backstage.)

[MUSIC NO. 2A: "MISTRESS QUICKLY"]

(ACTORS *prepare with a* **DOG. BURBAGE** *enters.)*

BURBAGE. Gentlemen of Verona. This is your two-minute call. Act One, Scene One. Wardrobe mistress, quickly.

MISTRESS QUICKLY. Ready, sir!

*(**WILL** arrives.)*

WILL. Burbage!

BURBAGE. Oh God, an author.

WILL. How dare you perform me here in front of the Queen without my say-so. I am still owed half of the commission.

BURBAGE. Not from me. I stole it from Henslowe. If he stole it from you that's his business.

WILL. Why is there a dog?

BURBAGE. The Queen loves a dog.

WILL. There's no dog in my *Two Gentlemen of Verona.*

BURBAGE. There is now.

WILL. I demand to be paid for this, Burbage.

BURBAGE. I told you I will make you a partner, Shakespeare. For fifty pounds. Your hireling days will be over.

WILL. Where will I go for fifty pounds?

BURBAGE. I hear Anne Hathaway is a woman of property.

WILL. No, she has a cottage. What would you give me for a comedy all but done?

BURBAGE. What's the part?

WILL. Romeo. Wit, swordsman, lover.

BURBAGE. And the title?

WILL. *Romeo.*

BURBAGE. I shall play him. Here's two sovereigns, and two more when you show me the pages. Now <u>begone</u>!

(**TILNEY** *appears.*)

TILNEY. My masters, are you mad? Her Majesty is waiting!

BURBAGE. We are ready, Mister Tilney.

TILNEY. Is that the dog?

BURBAGE. Yes.

TILNEY. But it's a different dog.

BURBAGE. The other was eaten by a bear.

TILNEY. The only reason the Queen asked to see this circus – was the dog.

ACTOR. But Spot can do tricks, sir, look. Spot, jump! Spot, jump!

(*The* **DOG** *fails to jump.*)

BURBAGE. I assure you he brings the house down at the Curtain.

TILNEY. It doesn't look funny.

BURBAGE. Nerves. He's never played the Palace.

TILNEY. If you don't go up this instant I will revoke your charter.

BURBAGE. Gentlemen. Beginners, please.

Scene Four

(Whitehall Palace.)

[MUSIC NO. 3: "VIVAT REGINA"]

(**QUEEN ELIZABETH**, *her* **ATTENDANTS**, *and the* **COURT** *are revealed as the play is about to begin.)*

QUEEN. Is this the one with the dog?

TILNEY. Yes, Your Majesty. *The Two Gentlemen of Verona*, an Italianate romance on the nature of love, with a dog.

QUEEN. Excellent. We very much liked the dog.

[MUSIC NO. 4: "TWO GENTS – UNDERSCORE"]

(Actors playing **VALENTINE** *and* **PROTEUS** *enter.)*

VALENTINE.

Cease to persuade, my loving Proteus.

Home-keeping youth have ever homely wits...

> *(The play continues in dumb-show as* **HENSLOWE** *meets* **WILL**.)*

HENSLOWE. I thought you'd be here. Where is my play? Shakespeare.

WILL. *(pointing to his head)* All locked safe in here.

HENSLOWE. Locked? I gave you three sovereigns a month ago.

WILL. Half what you owed me. I am still owed for one gentleman of Verona.

HENSLOWE. What is money to you and me? I am without a single new play while Burbage is invited here to Court and receives ten pounds to play your piece written for <u>my</u> theatre at <u>my</u> risk.

WILL. Mister Henslowe, will you lend me fifty pounds?

HENSLOWE. What for?

WILL. Burbage offers me a partnership in the Chamberlain's Men.

HENSLOWE. Cut out my heart – feed my liver to the dogs!

WILL. I'll take that as a no, then.

HENSLOWE. I'm a dead man and buggered to boot. I hear Burbage has a brand new Christopher Marlowe for the Curtain and I have nothing for the Rose. When will I get it, Will?

WILL. As soon as I have found my muse.

HENSLOWE. Who is it this time?

WILL. It is always Aphrodite.

HENSLOWE. Aphrodite Baggott who does it behind the Dog and Biscuit?

VALENTINE.

What light is light, if Silvia be not seen?
What joy is joy, if Silvia be not by?

(*The* **DOG** *enters and jumps up to* **VALENTINE**.)

Unless it be to think that she is by
And feed—

(*The* **DOG** *is causing problems.*)

—upon the shadow of perfection.

(*The* **QUEEN** *and the* **COURT** *laugh uproariously.* **BURBAGE** *enters.*)

BURBAGE. Spot! Spot! Out, damn Spot!

(**BURBAGE** *finally removes the* **DOG**. **HENSLOWE** *intently watches the audience.*)

HENSLOWE. See. Comedy. That's what they want. Love and a bit with a dog.

WILL. I refuse to watch this shambles.

(**WILL** *starts to leave.*)

HENSLOWE. Where are you going?

WILL. To hang myself. Ask for me tomorrow and you shall find me in a grave pit.

(**HENSLOWE** *stares at* **VIOLA** *in the audience as*
WILL *leaves.*)

HENSLOWE. Wait. There is a lady who knows your play by
heart. Look how she mouths the words. Will – Will…?

(**WILL** *has gone.*)

Scene Five

(De Lesseps Hall, Viola's bedroom.)

[MUSIC NO. 5: "BED ARRIVES"]

(VIOLA *is performing for an imaginary audience.)*

VIOLA.

What light is light, if Silvia be not seen?

What joy is joy, if Silvia be not by?

Unless it be to think that she is by

And feed upon the shadow of perfection.

MUSICIANS. *(sung)*

O, STAY AND HEAR! YOUR TRUE LOVE'S COMING,

THAT CAN SING BOTH HIGH AND LOW.

VIOLA.

Except I be by Silvia in the night,

There is no music in the nightingale;

Unless I look on Silvia in the day,

There is no day for me to look upon.

Such poetry…

*(Viola's **NURSE** enters.)*

…But how can one care for Silvia while she is – by the order of the Lord Chamberlain – played by a pipsqueak boy in petticoats!

NURSE. I liked the dog.

VIOLA. Stage love will never be real love until we women can be onstage ourselves. Yet when can we see another?

NURSE. When the Queen commands it.

VIOLA. But at the playhouse.

NURSE. Playhouses are not for well-born ladies.

VIOLA. I am not so well-born.

NURSE. Well-monied is the same as well-born these days and well-married better than both. Lord Wessex was looking at you tonight.

VIOLA. All the men at court are without poetry. If they look at me they see my father's fortune. I will have poetry in my life. And adventure. And love. Love above all.

NURSE. Like Valentine and Silvia?

VIOLA. No – not the artful postures of love, but the love that overthrows life. Unbiddable, ungovernable, like a riot in the heart, and nothing to be done, come ruin or rapture. Love like there has never been in a play. I will have love or I will end my days –

NURSE. As a nurse?

VIOLA. But I would be Valentine and Silvia too, somehow. Good Nurse, God save you and good night. I would stay asleep my whole life if I could dream myself into a company of players.

Scene Six

(Tavern.)

[MUSIC NO. 6: "TAVERN"]

(A **WAITER** *calls out while* **RALPH** *attends* **HENSLOWE**.*)*

WAITER. Calves' head with oysters and the coxcomb tartlet, table nine.

RALPH. Ah, Mister Henslowe. How goes it, sir?

HENSLOWE. Very well. Very well, Ralph, my good man. Some food and drink.

RALPH. Well, the special today is a pig's foot marinated in juniper berry vinegar served with a buckwheat pancake and a burdock salad.

HENSLOWE. I'll have a pie and pint. And have one for yourself, Master Ralph.

*(**FENNYMAN** enters with* **LAMBERT** *and* **FREES**.*)*

FENNYMAN. Next time we take your boots off.

LAMBERT. Get him!

FREES. Over the table, mate.

FENNYMAN. Stretch him!

HENSLOWE. Mister Fennyman. What have I done?

FENNYMAN. That is the question. Nothing. *(turning to the* **MUSICIANS**) Shut it! *(to* **HENSLOWE**) Why haven't you started?

HENSLOWE. Oh, it's all taken care of, gentlemen. It all takes time.

FENNYMAN. Where is the manuscript, Mister Henslowe?

HENSLOWE. A manuscript. Let me explain about the theatre business. The natural condition is one of insurmountable obstacles on the road to imminent disaster. One must never expect a manuscript at this stage. That is an impediment to look forward to. But it always works out in the end.

FENNYMAN. How?

HENSLOWE. I don't know. It's a mystery.

FENNYMAN. No pirates – you're a dead man. Come on.

>   (**FENNYMAN** *exits with* **LAMBERT** *and* **FREES**.)

>   *[MUSIC NO. 7: "TAVERN – UNDERSCORE"]*

RALPH. Did I hear you have a play, Mister Henslowe?

>   (**WILL** *enters and, avoiding* **HENSLOWE**, *makes his way to the bar.*)

HENSLOWE. Shakespeare is writing as we speak.

RALPH. Is there anything for me?

HENSLOWE. You're a perfect Pirate King, Ralph, but I hear you are a drunken sot.

RALPH. Never when I'm working.

>   (**NOL** *approaches.*)

NOL. What about me, Mister Henslowe?

HENSLOWE. And there's a nice little part for you, Master Nol.

NOL. Thank you very much.

RALPH. What about the money?

HENSLOWE. It won't cost you a penny. We will all share the profits. Auditions this afternoon.

WILL. Auditions?

HENSLOWE. Will.

WILL. Where are your usual men?

HENSLOWE. With Ned Alleyn in the provinces. God knows when they will return. We cannot delay. We need bodies, Will.

WILL. But not these pickled hams.

HENSLOWE. Auditions round the back in five minutes. If you are not there, Will, I will cast it myself. Ralph, bring the pie round.

> (HENSLOWE *leaves with* NOL *in tow.* WILL *goes to the bar.*)

WILL. Give me to drink mandragora.

> (MARLOWE *enters.*)

BARMAN. Straight up?

MARLOWE. Bring my friend a beaker of your best brandy.

BARMAN. Yes, Mister Marlowe.

MARLOWE. How goes it, Will?

WILL. Wonderful, wonderful. Most wonderful.

MARLOWE. Burbage says you're also writing him a play!

WILL. I have the chinks to show for it. *(puts down a coin for the drinks)* I insist, and a beaker for Mister Marlowe. And how is yours?

MARLOWE. Just finished. My best since *Faustus.*

WILL. I love your early work. This time?

MARLOWE. *The Massacre at Paris.* And yours?

WILL. *Romeo and Ethel the Pirate's Daughter. (off* MARLOWE*'s response)* Yes, I know.

MARLOWE. What's the story?

WILL. Well, there's this pirate…In truth I haven't written a word.

MARLOWE. Well, Romeo is…Italian.

WILL. Marvellous.

MARLOWE. Always in and out of love.

WILL. That's good. Until he meets…

MARLOWE. Ethel.

WILL. Really?

MARLOWE. Juliet.

WILL. Juliet?

MARLOWE. The daughter of his enemy.

WILL. The daughter of his enemy.

MARLOWE. His best friend is killed in a duel by Juliet's brother or something. His name is Mercutio.

WILL. Mercutio. Good name. What happens to Ethel?

MARLOWE. Marries a blackamoor and is strangled with a handkerchief?

WILL. Inspired. Thank you, Kit.

NOL. Will, Mister Henslowe is about to start the auditions for Romeo.

MARLOWE. I thought the play was for Burbage?

WILL. That's a different one.

MARLOWE. A different one you haven't written?

WILL. *(calling off)* Next!

Scene Seven

(Behind the tavern. Auditions.)

[MUSIC NO. 8: "AUDITIONS"]

(WILL and HENSLOWE watch ROBIN finish a musical piece.)

WILL. Thank you, and now for your modern piece.

ROBIN.

Was this the face that launched a thousand ships
And burnt the topless towers of Ilium?
Sweet Helen, make me immortal with a kiss.

WILL. Thank you. Next!

HENSLOWE. We have to cast somebody.

WILL. Next!

(ADAM enters.)

ADAM. I would like to give you something from *Faustus* by Christopher Marlowe.

WILL. How refreshing.

(ADAM begins an elaborate mime, opening and closing a door behind him.)

ADAM. *(fast and inaudibly)*

Was this the face that launched a thousand ships—

WILL. Next!

(WEBSTER comes in. WILL takes one look and dismisses him.)

Next!

WEBSTER. But I haven't started.

WILL. No doubt you will be giving us your Christopher Marlowe?

WEBSTER. Yes.

WILL. "The topless towers of Ilium"?

WEBSTER. No. *Tamburlaine the Great.*

WILL. Tamburlaine the Great was a bloodthirsty tyrant.
Not a ten-year-old malkin from Cheapside.

HENSLOWE. Maybe he could be Ethel.

WILL. This is absurd.

WEBSTER. *(plays Tamburlaine with vicious gusto)*
Go, villain, cast thee headlong from a rock,
Or rip thy bowels, and rent out thy heart,
T' appease my wrath; or else I'll torture thee,
Searing thy hateful flesh with burning irons...

WILL. Thank you!

WEBSTER.
And drops of scalding lead, while all thy joints
Be rack'd and beat asunder with the wheel.

WILL. Enough!

WEBSTER. I can do Barabas. Or the gory bit from the
Agamemnon.

WILL. We've seen enough.

> *(WEBSTER goes.)*

HENSLOWE. I liked him.

WILL. Next.

> *(WABASH enters.)*

HENSLOWE. Ah, Mister Wabash!

WABASH.
Was this the f-f-face that launched a thousand sh-sh-ships?

HENSLOWE. Very good, Mister Wabash. Excellent. Report
to the property master.

WABASH. Th-th-th-thank you very m-m-m-much.

> *(WABASH leaves.)*

HENSLOWE. My tailor. Wants to be an actor. I have a few debts here and there. Well, that seems to be everybody. Did you see a Romeo?

WILL. I did not.

HENSLOWE. Well, to my work, and you to yours. When can I see pages?

WILL. Tomorrow.

HENSLOWE. Tomorrow and...

WILL. Tomorrow.

> (**HENSLOWE** *leaves.* **VIOLA** *enters, dressed in men's clothing.*)

VIOLA/KENT. May I begin, sir?

WILL. Your name?

VIOLA/KENT. Thomas Kent. I would like to do a speech by a writer who commands the heart of every player, sir.

WILL. Yes, I am sure.

VIOLA/KENT.
What light is light, if Silvia be not seen?
What joy is joy, if Silvia be not by?
Unless it be to think that she is by,
And feed upon the shadow of perfection.
Except I be by Silvia in the night,
There is no music in the nightingale;
Unless I look on Silvia in the day,
There is no day for me to look upon.

WILL. Where did you learn to do that?

VIOLA/KENT. At the playhouse, sir.

WILL. There is no playhouse in London where my verse is spoke truly.

VIOLA/KENT. Are you Master Shakespeare?

WILL. I have not seen you audition before, Master Kent.

VIOLA/KENT. I am new to London, sir. I am from the country – staying at the de Lesseps'. In Cheam.

WILL. Please, sir. Speak some more. Without your hat.

VIOLA/KENT. My hat?

WILL. Let me see your face.

> (**WILL** *comes over to* **KENT** *and tries to remove his hat.*)

VIOLA/KENT. No!

WILL. Please. Speak it to me again. Let it trip off the tongue.

VIOLA/KENT. Sir!

WILL. It's a love scene. Please take off your hat.

> (**VIOLA** *continues to evade* **WILL**.)

VIOLA/KENT. Just leave my hat alone.

MARLOWE. *(entering)* Any luck?

> (**VIOLA** *runs straight into him.*)

Hello, young man.

> (**VIOLA** *escapes* **MARLOWE**'*s advance and leaves.*)

Who was he?

WILL. My Romeo. Hands off.

Scene Eight

(Outside De Lesseps Hall.)

[MUSIC NO. 9: "BALLROOM"]

(VIOLA, still dressed as KENT, runs in and encounters NURSE.)

NURSE. My Lady. Where have you been?

VIOLA. I have been to audition for the theatre.

NURSE. I'll be in my grave if they find out. Quick indoors, you must get ready for the ball. The guests are already arriving. Special guests, too, as well you should know. Your father is waiting to introduce you to Lord Wessex. You'll drive me to madness.

Scene Nine

(Inside De Lesseps Hall, decorated for a ball. The **COMPANY** *dances. Out of the action emerges a conversation between* **WESSEX** *and* **SIR ROBERT DE LESSEPS**.*)*

WESSEX. Where is she, Sir Robert? I am starting to wonder if she is a mythical beast of your invention.

DE LESSEPS. She will come, I assure you. She is a beauty, My Lord, as would take a king to church for a dowry of nutmeg.

WESSEX. My plantations in Virginia are not mortgaged for a nutmeg. I have an ancient name that will bring you preferment when your grandson is a Wessex. Is she fertile?

DE LESSEPS. She will breed. If she do not, send her back.

WESSEX. And obedient?

DE LESSEPS. As any mule in Christendom. But if you are the man to ride her, there are rubies in the saddle.

WESSEX. I like her.

DE LESSEPS. Come, she will be down any moment.

Scene Ten

(Gate outside De Lesseps Hall. **WILL** *appears with* **MARLOWE** *and is confronted by* **CATLING***, the guard.)*

CATLING. Sorry. You can't come in without an invite. This is a proper ball. For civilised people.

WILL. We are civilised people. I'm an actor and this is Christopher Marlowe, one of Europe's leading writers.

MARLOWE. Hello, young man.

CATLING. I don't care if you're bloody Beaumont and Fletcher, mates. You're not getting in without an invite.

WILL. But I have a letter. For Thomas Kent.

*(***NURSE*** appears.)*

NURSE. Who asks for Thomas Kent?

WILL. Will Shakespeare – actor, poet, and playwright of the Rose. Master Kent auditioned for me this afternoon.

NURSE. Master Kent?

WILL. You know him?

NURSE. Yes. He is my…nephew.

WILL. I have a letter. To offer him the lead part in my play.

NURSE. I will see that he gets it, sirs. Catling, let them through.

Scene Eleven

(Inside De Lesseps Hall.)

[MUSIC NO. 10: "PAVANE: WHAT IS LOVE?"]

(The **COMPANY** *dances.)*

MUSICIANS. *(sung)*

WHAT IS LOVE? 'TIS NOT HEREAFTER;

PRESENT MIRTH HATH PRESENT LAUGHTER;

WHAT'S TO COME IS STILL UNSURE:

YOUTH'S A STUFF WILL NOT ENDURE.

(Singing repeats quietly underneath the following conversations between **DE LESSEPS** *and* **WESSEX,** *and* **WILL, MARLOWE,** *and* **NURSE.** *Enter* **VIOLA.***)*

DE LESSEPS. My daughter.

WESSEX. Yes. I think she will do. She will do very nicely.

WILL. By all the stars in heaven, who is she?

NURSE. That's My Lady – Viola de Lesseps.

MARLOWE. Vain fantasy, Will Shakespeare.

WILL.

O, she doth teach the torches to burn bright.

MARLOWE.

So quick bright things come to confusion.

WILL. I will speak to her.

MARLOWE. We will be run out of here.

DE LESSEPS. Viola, My Lord Wessex.

WESSEX. Enchanted.

[MUSIC NO. 11: "MISS GIBSON'S ROUND"]

*(***WESSEX** *and* **VIOLA** *dance.)*

WESSEX. My Lady Viola.

VIOLA. My Lord.

WESSEX. I have spoken to your father.

VIOLA. So, My Lord. I speak with him every day.

WESSEX. I have spoken to your father about your future.

VIOLA. I trust you found it of interest. I rarely know what is going to happen next.

> (*As the dance turns,* **VIOLA** *realizes that* **WILL** *is dancing next to her as* **WESSEX** *moves on.*)

Good sir!

WILL. My Lady.

VIOLA. Are you not the poet William Shakespeare?

WILL. I am not, My Lady.

VIOLA. But sir, I have seen you at the playhouse.

WILL. I am a poet no longer. As I have seen a beauty that would prove all my poetry prose.

VIOLA. What brings you to my house?

WILL. I came to seek one who would make my words as fluent as the river. Now I find one who makes me dumb.

> (**VIOLA** *turns to* **WESSEX**.)

WESSEX. I need a dowry, your family seeks a title. It seems our fortunes are well met.

VIOLA. You think only of "a fortune," My Lord. Fate pays no heed to worldly commerce.

WESSEX. You mistake the times; finance and futures are inextricably linked.

> (**VIOLA** *turns to* **WILL**.)

WILL. This is a dream.

VIOLA.

Dreams are the children of an idle brain, begot of nothing but vain fantasy which is as thin of substance as the air.

WILL. Did you really just say that?

VIOLA. Indeed I truly hope, sir, this is no dream.

WILL. If we are awake let me dream you such words that will make you immortal.

VIOLA. Good sir. None can be immortal. I only dream of being alive.

WILL. Then I will be your poet.

(**WESSEX** *turns to* **WILL**.)

WESSEX. Poet? Nay, you are a knave, sir.

WILL. How do I offend, My Lord?

WESSEX. By coveting my property. I cannot shed blood in her house but I will cut your throat anon. You have a name, sirrah?

WILL. Christopher Marlowe, at your service.

(**WESSEX** *turns to* **VIOLA**.)

VIOLA. You smile, sir. I am glad you are happy.

WESSEX. I am perfectly happy, now.

Scene Twelve

(Viola's balcony. **NURSE** *finds* **VIOLA**.*)*

NURSE. Look, My Lady, a letter to Thomas Kent.

VIOLA. Who from?

NURSE. From the playwright, William Shakespeare.

[MUSIC NO. 12: "THE BALCONY"]

He was desperate to speak to "Master Kent."

VIOLA. Oh, I can't believe it. *(reads the letter)* "I have never heard my words spoken with such honesty. I am writing a comedy of quarrelling families reconciled in the discovery of Romeo to be the very same Capulet cousin stolen from the cradle and fostered to manhood by his Montague mother that was robbed of her own child by the Pirate King! And I would have you play Romeo Montague – a young gentleman of Verona."

NURSE. Verona, again?!

VIOLA. Is Master Shakespeare not handsome?

NURSE. He looks well enough for a mountebank.

VIOLA. Oh, Nurse! He would give Thomas Kent the life of Viola de Lesseps' dreaming.

NURSE. My Lady, this play will end badly.

VIOLA. 'Tis a comedy. It ends with a pirate jig. As you love me and as I love you, you will bind my breast and buy me a boy's wig. Rehearsals begin tomorrow.

NURSE. Your father—

VIOLA. From tomorrow away in the country for three weeks.

> **(MARLOWE** *and* **WILL** *have appeared under Viola's balcony.)*

MARLOWE. *(sotto voce)* Look. There she is. This is her balcony.

WILL. Oh, great heaven!

MARLOWE. Go on and speak to her.

WILL. I don't dare! The nurse is there.

NURSE. My Lady. You'll catch your death out here.

VIOLA. Leave me, Nursey.

NURSE. Believe me, this will all end in tears.

(NURSE exits. VIOLA reads the letter again.)

VIOLA. Romeo, Romeo…a young gentleman of Verona. A comedy. By William Shakespeare.

MARLOWE. Well, go on. *(shoves WILL)* My Lady.

VIOLA. Who is there?

WILL. Will Shakespeare.

NURSE. *(offstage)* Madam!

VIOLA. Anon, good Nurse, anon. Master Shakespeare?

WILL. The same, alas.

VIOLA. Why alas?

WILL. A lowly player.

VIOLA. Alas indeed, for I thought you the highest poet of my esteem and a writer of the most brilliant comedies that capture my heart.

WILL. Oh – I am him too.

NURSE. *(offstage)* Lady Viola.

VIOLA. Anon, good Nurse, anon. *(to WILL)* I will come again.

(VIOLA goes in to deal with NURSE.)

MARLOWE. Enough. She takes the bait, let's go.

WILL. Nonsense. I'm just getting somewhere.

MARLOWE. "A lowly player"?! You're supposed to be a poet. Get out of there before you shame us all.

(VIOLA returns.)

VIOLA. If they find you here, they will kill you.

WILL. And you can bring them with a word.

VIOLA. Not for the world! Speak to me. Inspire me.

WILL. *(trying rather pathetically to be poetic)* Alas I cannot for I am…struck dumb by your beauty.

VIOLA. Come, come. Good poet. These are hackneyed tropes. Extemporise, improvise. Fill me with your words.

MARLOWE. Leave.

WILL. *(to* **VIOLA***)* Now?

VIOLA. Yes. Translate our base tongue into the golden verse of love.

WILL. Erm… *(under his breath)* Pigs!

VIOLA. What was that?

MARLOWE. Recite something you know.

WILL. I've gone blank.

MARLOWE. Anything.

WILL. Help me, Kit!

MARLOWE. "Shall I compare thee…?"

WILL.

Shall I compare thee to a summer's day?
Thou art more lovely and more temperate.

MARLOWE. Well, it's not exactly Philip Sidney.

VIOLA. Go on.

WILL. *(to* **MARLOWE***)* That's as far as I got.

MARLOWE. As far as you got?!

WILL. Help me, Kit!

MARLOWE.

Rough winds…

WILL.

Rough winds…

MARLOWE.

Do shake...

WILL.

Do shake...

MARLOWE.

The darling buds of...May.

WILL. Isn't that spring?

MARLOWE. It rhymes with "day."

WILL.

The darling buds of...May.

MARLOWE.

And summer's lease...

WILL.

And summer's lease...

MARLOWE.

Hath all too short a date.

WILL.

Hath all too short a date.

VIOLA. Oh this is beautiful, Will... More...

MARLOWE. Dum di dum di dum di...got it...

But thy eternal summer...

WILL. *(repeating as he goes)*

But thy eternal summer...

MARLOWE.

Shall not fade...

WILL.

Shall not fade...

MARLOWE.

Nor lose possession of that fair thou owest...

WILL.

Nor lose possession of that fair thou owest...

MARLOWE.

Nor shall death…

WILL. Don't mention death…

MARLOWE. Death is good.

WILL.

Nor shall death…

MARLOWE.

Brag thou wandrest in his shade.

WILL.

Brag thou wandrest in his shade.

MARLOWE.

When in eternal lines to time thou growest.

WILL. *(to* **MARLOWE***)* What does that mean?

MARLOWE. Just say it.

WILL.

When in eternal lines to time thou growest.

MARLOWE.

So long as men can breathe…

WILL.

So long as men can breathe,

(adding his own bit) or eyes can see…

MARLOWE. Not bad…

WILL. *(now inspired)*

So long lives this…

MARLOWE. That's it.

WILL.

…and this gives life to thee.

MARLOWE. Bravo.

WILL. I have it back, Kit.

VIOLA. Oh, it's beautiful.

WILL. It's nothing, really.

VIOLA. Only you could have conceived such a thing.

WILL. I think it lacks something in the middle.

VIOLA. Not another word. It's perfect.

NURSE. *(offstage)* Madam.

VIOLA. I must go.

WILL. No. But I am a poor poet. I have not had payment.

VIOLA. Such sublime eloquence is God's own recompense.

WILL.

Yet to receive the prayers of those two pilgrims – thy lips...

MARLOWE. Too far.

VIOLA. I could not sully thy lips gilded with such golden words.

WILL. Lady, you will burnish them to brighter eloquence. *(to* **MARLOWE***)* Help me up, Kit.

> *(***WILL*** gets on* **MARLOWE***'s shoulders.)*

VIOLA. Good sir, do not use yourself all up.

WILL.

With love's light wings, did I o'er perch these walls...

MARLOWE. God, you're heavy!

WILL.

For stony limits cannot hold love out,

And what love can do, that dares love attempt.

Therefore thy kinsmen are no stop to me.

MARLOWE. Very good.

WILL. Thank you.

> *(***WILL*** struggles with* **MARLOWE***'s help to get up onto the balcony.)*

NURSE. Lady Viola!

VIOLA. Oh, go away!

NURSE. Your father comes.

[MUSIC NO. 13: "ALARM"]

(**VIOLA** *goes in.* **WILL** *pulls himself up.*)

WILL. *(to himself)* I am fortune's fool – I will be punished for this.

MARLOWE. Jump!

WILL. Hang on, I'm just getting the hang of this.

(**NURSE** *re-enters, comes face-to-face with* **WILL,** *and screams.*)

VOICES. What ho! Lights!

(**WILL** *jumps just in time.* **GUARDS** *enter with* **WESSEX.**)

GUARD 1. Where did they go?

GUARD 2. They went that way.

GUARD 1. Which way?

WESSEX. You that way. You this way. Now go!!

Scene Thirteen

(The Rose Theatre. Rehearsals – day one.)

FENNYMAN. Is this it?

HENSLOWE. Yes.

FENNYMAN. Is this a rehearsal?

HENSLOWE. Yes.

FENNYMAN. Is it always like this?

HENSLOWE. Yes.

FENNYMAN. Is it going well?

HENSLOWE. Very well.

FENNYMAN. But nothing seems to be happening.

HENSLOWE. Exactly. But it's all happening very well.

*(**WILL** comes on and hands **RALPH** his "part.")*

FENNYMAN. Who's that?

HENSLOWE. Nobody. The author.

FENNYMAN. If this doesn't work, Henslowe, you are forcemeat.

HENSLOWE. Will, Will! It starts well, but then it gets all long-faced. Where's the comedy, Will? Where's the dog? Do you think it's funny?

RALPH. I was a Pirate King, now I'm a Nurse. That's funny.

HENSLOWE. We are at least four acts short, Will.

WILL. We are short of any discernible acting talent – those that we have are over-parted ranters and stutterers who should be sent back to the stocks. Let's wait for Ned Alleyn. We can't even be sure we have a Romeo.

*(**WEBSTER** comes on.)*

Who are you?

WEBSTER. I'm Ethel, sir, the pirate's daughter.

WILL. *(to **HENSLOWE**)* I'm damned if he is!

HENSLOWE. I think he has potential.

WILL. This is a shambles.

HENSLOWE. I think we should get started.

WILL. Gentlemen! Good men all.

HENSLOWE. *(to* **FENNYMAN***)* It is customary to make a little speech on the first day. It does no harm and the authors like it.

WILL. Firstly, gentlemen, I want to thank you all for coming here today. I am honoured to be working with such an extraordinary calibre of actor. Today we are about to embark upon a mysterious journey, a journey which—

FENNYMAN. I'll speak the speech.

WILL. I haven't quite finished.

FENNYMAN. Shut it! Now you listen to me, you dregs! Actors are ten a penny and I, Hugh Fennyman, hold your nuts in my hand so—

> *(Noise from offstage. Suddenly, a group of* **ACTORS** *enter, headed by* **NED ALLEYN** *– a handsome, piratical figure with a big voice.)*

NED. Huzzah! I am returned!

FENNYMAN. Excuse me, I was speaking the speech.

NED. Silence, you dog. I hear there is a play for me.

FENNYMAN. Who are you, sir?

NED. Who am I? I am Hieronimo! I am Tamburlaine! I am Faustus! I am Barabas the Jew – oh yes, Master Will, and I was Henry the Sixth – several times. *(to* **FENNYMAN***)* Who are you, sir?

FENNYMAN. I am the money.

NED. Then you may remain, as long as you remain silent. Congratulations, sir. Your investment is safe in the hands of…

ACTORS. Ned Alleyn!

NED. What is the play? What is my part?

WILL. We are in desperate want of a Mercutio, Ned, a young nobleman of Verona.

NED. Verona, again. And what is the title?

WILL. *Mercutio.*

NED. I will play him! Divide the rest betwixt the boys and watch how genius creates a legend.

WILL. *(handing out parts)* Master Pope! Master Phillips! Master Hemmings! Master Condell! Master Tooley! Master Wabash! Master Nol! Sam, my pretty one! Are you ready to fall in love again?

SAM. I am, Master Shakespeare.

WILL. But your voice…have they dropped?

SAM. No, no, a touch of cold.

FENNYMAN. Actually, Master Shakespeare, I saw his Tamburlaine. Wonderful.

WILL. Oh, yes…

FENNYMAN. Of course, it was mighty writing. There is no one quite like Marlowe.

WILL. No indeed. Mister Henslowe, you have your actors. Except for Thomas Kent. *(to **WEBSTER**)* Are you still here, boy?

WEBSTER. I was in one of your plays before. They cut my head off in *Titus Andronicus*. When I write plays they will be like *Titus*.

WILL. You liked it?

WEBSTER. No. But I like it when they cut heads off. And the daughter mutilated with knives. Plenty of blood. That's the only writing.

NED. Will…where is Mercutio?

WILL. I am saving my best for him. I leave the scene in your safe-keeping, Ned. Cut round – what's his name – Romeo, for now.

NED. Who?

WILL. Nobody. Mercutio's friend. *(turns to find* **KENT***)* Master Kent! I almost didn't recognise you.

HENSLOWE. Places, please.

NED. Gather around, gentlemen.

(Enter **BURBAGE***.)*

BURBAGE. Shakespeare!

HENSLOWE. Oh God!

BURBAGE. You cur. I thought I'd find you here. Where's Ethel?

WILL. Who?

BURBAGE. The pirate's daughter I paid two sovereigns for… *(sees* **NED***)* Mister Alleyn.

NED. Mister Burbage.

BURBAGE. The Prince of the Provinces.

NED. The Scourge of the Suburbs.

BURBAGE. Where is my play, Shakespeare? I have postered half of Shoreditch and I haven't seen a single page.

WILL. They're coming, they're coming.

BURBAGE. If you've sold my play to Henslowe I will slice you nape to chops. What play is this, Alleyn?

NED. *Mercutio.*

HENSLOWE. Out of this theatre, you over-ripe ham. We are trying to rehearse.

BURBAGE. My play, Shakespeare, or I will do such things – I know not what they are – but they shall be the terrors of all Shoreditch.

(Exit **BURBAGE***.)*

NED. …they shall be the terrors of all Shoreditch…

HENSLOWE. Gentlemen. Romeo laments his Ethel.

WILL. May I, Mister Alleyn?

(**NED** *nods.*)

Master Kent is playing Romeo, and Master Nol is
Benvolio. Gentlemen, a scene in Verona.

VIOLA/ROMEO.

Ay me, sad hours seem long.

Was that my father that went hence so fast?

NOL/BENVOLIO.

It was. What sadness lengthens Romeo's hours?

VIOLA/ROMEO.

Not having that which, having, makes them short.

HENSLOWE. He's good.

NOL/BENVOLIO.

In love?

VIOLA/ROMEO.

Out.

NOL/BENVOLIO.

Of love?

VIOLA/ROMEO. *(over-acting)*

Out of her favour where I am in love.

WILL. No no! Don't spend it all at once! He is speaking
about a baggage we never even meet! What will be left
in your purse when he meets his Juliet? What will you
do in Act Two when he meets the love of his life?

VIOLA/KENT. I am very sorry, sir, I have not seen Act Two.

WILL. Of course. It is not yet written. At a ball – Sam, will
you come down? – he sees the most beautiful girl in
Verona. All thoughts of Ethel, all thoughts of anything,
are wiped from his mind and he can think only of
her. At the ball they meet, they share a moment but
are torn asunder. That night he steals to her balcony.
And in the darkness he looks to the window – he sees
a torch and woos her with a transport of poetry – "But
soft, what light through yonder window breaks? It is
the east and Juliet is the sun."

SAM. It's beautiful.

WILL. "Arise fair sun…"

HENSLOWE. What about Ethel? I paid for a pirate's daughter.

WILL. Patience. All will come together.

VIOLA/KENT. Does Romeo get his Juliet?

WILL. Of course. It is a comedy.

FENNYMAN. Enough "speaky speaky." Let's get on with it.

HENSLOWE. From the top.

NED. Gentlemen. Capulets stage left, Montagues stage right. And square up.

> *(As **ACTORS** set their positions, **WILL** steals a private word with **KENT**.)*

WILL. Thomas, Master Kent, I have a letter for Lady Viola de Lesseps. The lady of your house. You know her?

VIOLA/KENT. As well as I know myself, sir. What is it about?

WILL. Fourteen lines. Give it to her. I shall ever be in your debt.

> *(**WILL** leaves. Transition.)*

> *[MUSIC NO. 14: "LETTER – UNDERSCORE"]*

VIOLA. Oh, it is complete. *(reads)*

Shall I compare thee to a summer's day?
Thou art more lovely and more temperate.
Rough winds do shake the darling buds of May,
And summer's lease hath all too short a date.

Sometime too hot the eye of heaven shines,
And often is his gold complexion dimm'd;
And every fair from fair some time declines,
By chance, or nature's changing course untrimm'd:
But thy eternal summer shall not fade

Nor lose possession of that fair thou ow'st,

Nor shall Death brag thou wander'st in his shade
When in eternal lines to time thou grow'st.
So long as men can breathe or eyes can see,
So long lives this, and this gives life to thee.

[END MUSIC NO. 14]
Oh, I am made immortal!

Scene Fourteen

(De Lesseps Hall.)

[MUSIC NO. 15: "INTO BEDROOM"]

(VIOLA is still in her costume. NURSE enters.)

NURSE. My Lady. My Lady. My Lady. Where have you been? Lord Wessex is waiting for you. He's waiting downstairs. Quickly, you must change.

(VIOLA runs offstage to change.)

VIOLA. *(from offstage)* How long has he been here?

NURSE. All morning.

VIOLA. What did you tell him?

NURSE. I told him you were at prayer, My Lady.

VIOLA. For four hours?

NURSE. I said you were pious, My Lady.

VIOLA. Why is he here today?

NURSE. You know perfectly well, My Lady.

(Enter WESSEX.)

WESSEX. Nurse. Nurse! Where is the future Lady Wessex?

NURSE. You must have patience, sir. My Lady is still in the act of contemplation.

WESSEX. Lengthy orisons for one so young.

NURSE. She always was a pious little girl, My Lord. My mistress is the sweetest lady, My Lord, and still as pious. Lord, Lord, even when she was a prating child, sir, she would spend hours on her knees. I used to swear she'd wear them out!

WESSEX. Oh, for heaven's sake, where the devil is she?!

(VIOLA runs back on, fully dressed.)

NURSE. My Lady, My Lady, Lord Wessex is here...

(Just in time, NURSE whips off VIOLA's moustache.)

WESSEX. My Lady.

VIOLA. Lord Wessex. You have been waiting.

WESSEX. I am aware of it. It is beauty's privilege. Though four hours' prayer is less piety than self-importance. I have spoken to the Queen. Her Majesty's consent is requisite when a Wessex takes a wife, and once gained, her consent is her command.

VIOLA. Do you intend to marry, My Lord?

WESSEX. Your father should keep you better informed. He has bought me for you. He returns from his estates to see us married two weeks from Saturday. You are allowed to show your pleasure.

VIOLA. But I do not love you, My Lord.

WESSEX. How your mind hops about! Your father was a shopkeeper, your children will bear a coat of arms, and I will recover my fortune. That is the only matter under discussion today. You will like Virginia.

VIOLA. Virginia?

WESSEX. Why, yes! My fortune lies in my plantations. The tobacco weed. I need four thousand pounds to fit out a ship and put my investments to work – I fancy tobacco has a future. We will not stay there long, three or four years.

VIOLA. But why me?

WESSEX. It was your eyes. No, your lips.

> (**WESSEX** *kisses* **VIOLA** *with more passion than ceremony.* **VIOLA** *slaps him.*)

Will you defy your father and your Queen?

VIOLA. The Queen has consented?

WESSEX. She wants to inspect you. At Greenwich, come Sunday. Be submissive, modest, grateful. And on time.

> (**WESSEX** *leaves.*)

VIOLA. My summer's lease is all too brief. Bring me pen and ink. I must write to William Shakespeare.

Scene Fifteen

(The Rose Theatre. Rehearsals. The **COMPANY**
assemble.)

WILL. Gentlemen. New pages!

[MUSIC NO. 16: "NEW PAGES"]

*(**WILL** hands out new pages.)*

NED. Will, hold. Can I have a word?

WILL. You do not like the speech?

NED. The speech is excellent.

NED & WILL. "O, then I see Queen Mab hath been with
you."

NED. Excellent and a good length. But then he disappears
for the length of a Bible.

WILL. But then you have his duel, a skirmish of words and
swords such as I never wrote, nor any man. He dies
with such a passion and poetry as you ever read – "A
plague on both your houses!"

NED. He dies!?

HENSLOWE. There doesn't appear to be a dog of any kind?

WILL. There was never going to be a dog.

HENSLOWE. I've just bought it from Will Kemp for three
sovereigns. And it's eating me out of house and home.

WILL. I will try to work one in.

FENNYMAN. Shut it. I want to hear what happens next.
Author, please.

WILL. The Friar marries the lovers in secret, then Ned,
playing Mercutio, gets into a fight with one of the
Capulets called Tybalt. Romeo—

*(**WEBSTER** volunteers himself.)*

—in your dreams – tries to stop them, he gets in
Mercutio's way, so Tybalt slays Mercutio and then
Romeo slays Tybalt.

FENNYMAN. Wonderful!

WILL. Then the Prince banishes Romeo from Verona.

HENSLOWE. And that's when he goes on the voyage and gets shipwrecked on the island of the Pirate King. Who has a dog!

FENNYMAN. Enough! Cease your prattling. This is not just entertainment. This is art.

HENSLOWE. But I paid Will Kemp three sovereigns for that cruel-hearted cur.

FENNYMAN. Shut it. And then…?

WILL. And then…it all works out in the end.

FENNYMAN. Masterful.

(VIOLA, *as* KENT, *comes in, flustered and late.*)

HENSLOWE. Ah, Master Kent. You've kindly decided to join us.

VIOLA/KENT. Sorry, there was a terrible snarl-up under Putney Bridge.

FENNYMAN. Right. Now you're here let's get on with it.

(*As the* COMPANY *take their positions,* NED *calls* WILL *over.*)

NED. Will…

WILL. I know, I know.

NED. It's good.

WILL. Oh.

NED. But the title. *Romeo and Juliet.* Just a suggestion.

WILL. Thank you, Ned… You are a gentleman.

NED. And you are a Warwickshire shithouse. (*to the* COMPANY) The Capulet ball. The dancing begins.

FENNYMAN. Places, please.

[*MUSIC NO. 17: "DANCE REHEARSAL 1"*]

(*The* ACTORS *dance as* NED *gives direction.*)

NED. Gentlemen, keep time, distance, proportion. Ready. And. Double forward. And double back. Turn, face your partner. Double away...The lovers touch hands... That's good...Next figure. Leaving the lovers...

VIOLA/ROMEO.

If I profane with my unworthiest hand,

This holy shrine, the gentle sin is this;

My lips, two blushing pilgrims, ready stand,

To smooth that rough touch with a tender kiss.

SAM/JULIET.

Good pilgrim, you do wrong your hand too much,

Which mannerly devotion shows in this;

For saints have hands that pilgrims' hands do touch,

And palm to palm is holy palmers' kiss.

VIOLA/ROMEO.

Have not saints lips, and holy palmers too?

SAM/JULIET.

Ay, pilgrim, lips that they must use in prayer.

VIOLA/ROMEO.

O, then, dear saint, let lips do what hands do!

They pray; grant thou, lest faith turn to despair.

SAM/JULIET.

Saints do not move, though grant for prayers' sake.

(VIOLA *is distracted by* WILL.)

It's your cue.

VIOLA/ROMEO.

Then move not while my prayer's effect I take.

(VIOLA *kisses* SAM *demurely on the cheek.*)

WILL. Stop! What was that? *(to* NED*)* Sorry, Mister Alleyn.

NED. Carry on, Mister Shakespeare.

WILL. Master Kent, you kiss like a child. If there is no sin, there is no trespass. Observe. Sam, what was the line?

SAM. "Then move not while my prayer's effect I take."

WILL/ROMEO.

Then move not while my prayer's effect I take.

>   (**WILL** *kisses* **SAM** *passionately.*)

WILL & SAM. *(to* **KENT***)* You see?

WILL. Thank you, Ned. Go back.

>   *[MUSIC NO. 18: "DANCE REHEARSAL 2"]*
>
>   *(The dance recommences.)*

SAM/JULIET.

Saints do not move though grant for prayers' sake.

VIOLA/ROMEO.

Then move not while my prayer's effect I take.

>   (**SAM** *and* **VIOLA** *kiss again, almost as demurely.*)

WILL. *(exploding)* Where is the danger? You are consorting with your family's mortal enemy. Now I am Juliet. Let's carry on with the scene.

>   *[MUSIC NO. 19: "DANCE REHEARSAL 3"]*
>
>   *(The dance starts again.)*

VIOLA/ROMEO.

Thus from my lips, by thine, my sin is purged.

WILL/JULIET.

Then have my lips the sin that they have took.

VIOLA/ROMEO.

Sin from my lips? O trespass sweetly urg'd!

Give me my sin again.

>   (**VIOLA** *hesitates then kisses* **WILL** *passionately. It becomes an extravagant display.*)

NED. *(as they continue to kiss)* Thank you – problem solved.

WILL. Much better, Master Kent.

NED. Let's skip to the end of the scene. *(reads)* "Exeunt Capulet, Lady Capulet, Guests, Gentlewomen and Masquers."

VIOLA/KENT. Will, I have a letter for you from Viola de Lesseps.

>   (**RALPH** and **SAM** begin to rehearse. **VIOLA** exits.)

SAM/JULIET.

> Come hither, Nurse. What is yond gentleman?
> Go ask his name. If he be married,
> My grave is like to be my wedding bed.

RALPH/NURSE.

> His name is Romeo, and a Montague,
> The only son of your great enemy.

>   [MUSIC NO. 20: "WILL READS VIOLA'S LETTER –
>   UNDERSCORE"]

>   (**WILL** opens and reads the letter as **VIOLA** appears
>   and gives voice to her words.)

MUSICIAN. (sung under the following line)
>   O MISTRESS MINE, WHERE ARE YOU ROAMING?

VIOLA. William, I am to be married to Lord Wessex a week on Saturday. Do not come to the house, it is dangerous for you. Please do not visit me again.

>   (**VIOLA** disappears. We are back in rehearsal.)

PETER/TYBALT.

> Juliet! Juliet!

NED. No, no, no. Too early. He's not finished yet. Are you all right, Will? Carry on.

SAM/JULIET.

> Of one I danced withal.

RALPH/NURSE.

> Anon, anon!
> Come, let's away; the strangers all are gone.

WILL. (still reading the letter) Purgatory, torture, hell itself.

>   [END MUSIC NO. 20]

RALPH. I weren't that bad.

WILL. Master Kent!

> (**WILL** *runs offstage.*)

Scene Sixteen

*(The river. A boat with **BOATMAN** at the bank.
VIOLA enters, still dressed as **KENT**.)*

VIOLA/KENT. Boatman. Down river. De Lesseps Hall,
please. On the double.

[MUSIC NO. 21: "DOWNRIVER"]

*(**VIOLA** climbs aboard. The boat is about to pull
away when **WILL** comes on, running.)*

WILL. Thomas! Thomas! Wait! Thomas!

*(**WILL** jumps on.)*

BOATMAN. Steady on, guvnor.

VIOLA/KENT. Will!

WILL. I have to speak with you.

BOATMAN. Hang on a minute. I know your face. You're an
actor. I saw you in something.

WILL. Very possibly.

BOATMAN. What was it? The one with a king?

VIOLA/KENT. Please, I'm in a hurry.

BOATMAN. I had that Christopher Marlowe in the back of
my boat once.

*(The **BOATMAN** pulls away.)*

WILL. Oh, Thomas, I am undone, my strings are cut – I'm
a puppet in a box.

BOATMAN. Writer as well, are you?

WILL & VIOLA/KENT. Row your boat!

[MUSIC NO. 22: "THE ROWBOAT"]

WILL. *(pulls out the letter)* She tells me to keep away. She is
to marry Lord Wessex.

VIOLA/KENT. If you love her, you must do as she asks.

WILL. And break her heart and mine?

VIOLA/KENT. It's only yours you can know.

WILL. She loves me, Thomas!

VIOLA/KENT. Does she say so?

WILL. Well, no…And yet she does. Look where the ink has run with tears. Was she weeping when she gave you this?

VIOLA/KENT. I…Her letter came to me by the nurse.

WILL. Your aunt?

VIOLA/KENT. Yes, my aunt. Perhaps she wept a little. Tell me how you love her, Will.

WILL. Like a sickness and its cure together.

VIOLA/KENT. Yes, like rain and sun, like cold and heat. *(collecting herself)* Is your lady beautiful? Since I came to visit from the country, I have not seen her close. Tell me, is she beautiful?

WILL. Oh, Thomas, if I could write the beauty of her eyes! I was born to look in them and know myself.

VIOLA/KENT. And her lips?

WILL. Oh, Thomas, her lips! The early morning rose would wither on the branch, if it could feel envy!

VIOLA/KENT. And her voice? Like lark song?

WILL. Deeper, softer. None of your twittering larks! I would banish nightingales from her garden before they interrupt her song.

VIOLA/KENT. She sings too?

WILL. Constantly. Without doubt. And plays the lute, she has a natural ear. And her bosom – Thomas, Thomas, did I mention her bosom?

VIOLA/KENT. What of her bosom?

WILL. Oh, Thomas, a pair of pippins! As round and rare as golden apples.

VIOLA/KENT. I think the lady is wise to keep your love at a distance. For what lady could live up to it close to, when her eyes and lips and voice may be no more beautiful than mine? Besides, can a lady born to wealth and noble marriage love happily with a bankside poet and player?

WILL. Yes, by God! Love knows nothing of rank or riverbank! It will spark between a queen and the poor vagabond who plays the king, and their love should be minded by each, for love denied blights the soul we owe to God! So tell My Lady, William Shakespeare waits for her in the garden.

VIOLA/KENT. But what of Lord Wessex?

WILL. For one kiss I would defy a thousand Wessexes!

VIOLA/KENT. Oh, Will.

> *[END MUSIC NO. 22]*

> *(VIOLA kisses WILL, then runs off, paying the BOATMAN as she goes.)*

WILL. Wait. Thomas.

BOATMAN. Thanks, M'Lady.

WILL. Lady?!

BOATMAN. Viola de Lesseps. Knew her since she was this high. Always a bit of a tomboy. But the facial hair is a big surprise.

> *(WILL is in shock.)*

Strangely enough I'm a bit of a writer myself.

> *(The BOATMAN produces a brick-sized manuscript and hands it to WILL.)*

It wouldn't take you long to read it. 'Spect you know all the booksellers…

> *[MUSIC NO. 23: "PAVANE TO BEDROOM"]*

> *(WILL steps out of the boat as the BOATMAN rows off. WILL tosses the manuscript into the river and follows VIOLA.)*

Scene Seventeen

MUSICIANS. *(sung)*
> WHAT IS LOVE? 'TIS NOT HEREAFTER;
> PRESENT MIRTH HATH PRESENT LAUGHTER;
> WHAT'S TO COME IS STILL UNSURE:
> YOUTH'S A STUFF WILL NOT EDURE.

> *(Viola's bedroom.* **VIOLA** *runs in, distraught.* **WILL** *follows.)*

WILL. Thomas? Viola? O brave new world! Are you my actor or my muse?

VIOLA. I am both but should be neither.

WILL. Can you love a fool?

VIOLA. Can you love a player?

WILL. If he is made like you.

> *(***WILL*** *gently takes off* **VIOLA***'s moustache.)*

VIOLA. Sir, I am a lady.

> *(They are about to kiss.)*

WILL. Wait! You are still a maid and perhaps mistook in me as I was mistook in Thomas Kent.

VIOLA. Are you not the author of the plays of William Shakespeare?

WILL. I am.

VIOLA. Then kiss me for I am not mistook.

> *(They kiss.)*

VIOLA. You have bound me to you.

WILL. Then let me unbind thee.

> *(***WILL*** *tries to take off* **VIOLA***'s jacket to unwind her binding but she takes pages from his pocket.)*

VIOLA. What is this?

WILL. Nothing.

VIOLA. What are these pages?

WILL. They can wait.

VIOLA. No, I must see them. *(reads)*

> *[MUSIC NO. 24: "THE BEDROOM"]*

But soft! What light through yonder window breaks?
Is it the East, and Juliet is the sun!
Arise, fair sun, and kill the envious moon,
Who is already sick and pale with grief
That thou her maid art far more fair than she.

Oh, Will!

WILL. Do you like it?

VIOLA.

The brightness of her cheek would shame those stars
As daylight doth a lamp...

You—

WILL.

See how she leans her cheek upon her hand!
O that I were a glove upon that hand,
That I might touch that cheek!

VIOLA.

Ay me!

This is wondrous.

WILL. *(from memory)*

She speaks.

O, speak again, bright angel...

VIOLA. *(reading)*

Romeo, Romeo! Wherefore art thou Romeo?

WILL.

O, be some other name!

VIOLA.

> What's in a name? That which we call a rose
> By any other word would smell as sweet.
> Romeo, doff thy name;
> And for thy name, which is no part of thee,
> Take all myself.
>
>> *(Reads on.)*
>
> I take thee at thy word.
> Call me but love, and I'll be new baptised.
>
> Sweet Montague, be true.
> Stay but a little, I will come again.

WILL.

> O blessed, blessed night! I am afeard,
> Being in night, all this is but a dream,
> Too flattering-sweet to be substantial.

VIOLA. She leaves?

WILL. But returns. I came on something. The friar who marries them will take up their destinies.

VIOLA. So it will end well for love?

WILL. In heaven perhaps. It is not a comedy I am writing now.

VIOLA. A tragedy?

WILL. Come, there will be time for plays.

VIOLA. Wait. There is more.

> I would I were thy bird.
> Sweet, so would I.
> Yet I should kill thee with much cherishing.
>
> My bounty is as boundless as the sea...

WILL & VIOLA.

> My love as deep.

WILL.

The more I give to thee,

The more I have. For both are infinite.

(**WILL** *and* **VIOLA** *dive into bed.*)

End of Act One

ACT TWO

Scene One

[MUSIC NO. 25: "SHALL I COMPARE THEE"]

MUSICIANS. *(sung)*

> SHALL I COMPARE THEE TO A SUMMER'S DAY?
> THOU ART MORE LOVELY AND MORE TEMPERATE.
> ROUGH WINDS DO SHAKE THE DARLING BUDS OF MAY,
> AND SUMMER'S LEASE HATH ALL TOO SHORT A DATE.
> TOO SHORT A DATE.

> *(Viola's bedroom. The bed-curtains are closed.
> Coital noises emerge from within, louder and
> louder until climax.)*

VIOLA. *(still out of breath)* I would not have thought it.
There is something better than a play.

WILL. There is?

VIOLA. Even your play.

WILL. Well, perhaps better than *Two Gentlemen of Verona.*

VIOLA. And that was only my first try.

> *(The bed-curtains open.)*

You would not leave me?

WILL. I must. Look – how pale the window.

VIOLA. Moonlight.

WILL. You're right – let Henslowe wait.

VIOLA. Henslowe?!

WILL. Let him be damned for his pages!

VIOLA. Oh, no. No.

WILL. There is time. It is still dark.

VIOLA. It is broad day. The cockerel tells us so.

WILL. It was the owl. Believe me, love, it was the owl.

VIOLA. You would leave us players without a scene to read today?

NURSE. *(offstage)* My Lady.

VIOLA. Go away!

> *(They shut the bed-curtains. **NURSE** enters with Viola's clothes in a large laundry basket.)*

NURSE. *(sung)*

O MISTRESS MINE, WHERE ARE YOU ROAMING?

O, STAY AND HEAR! YOUR TRUE LOVE'S COMING.

My Lady. It is a new day.

VIOLA. It is a new world.

NURSE. My Lady…it is Sunday. You are already due at Greenwich…to meet the Queen. *(sings)*

TRIP NO FURTHER, PRETTY SWEETING.

> *(**NURSE** opens the curtains and sees **WILL**. A pause.)*

(sentimentally) Ahhh.

WESSEX. *(offstage)* Where is she? Damn you.

NURSE. My Lady! Lord Wessex awaits.

WESSEX. Out of my way! *(appearing, to **NURSE**)* I demand that she to be brought to me.

> *(**NURSE** leaves **WILL** to help **VIOLA** get dressed, and goes to **WESSEX**.)*

NURSE. Hold your horses, My Lord. I'm coming as fast as I can. As my mother used to say, patience is a virtue. Be patient, My Lord, she is dressing.

WESSEX. Will you ask Her Majesty to be patient? The Queen Gloria Regina, God's Chosen Vessel, the

Radiant One, who shines her light on us, is at Greenwich today, and prepared, during the evening's festivities, to bestow her gracious favour on my choice of wife – and if we're late the old boot will not forgive. So either you produce her with or without her undergarments or I will drag her out myself.

NURSE. Of course, My Lord, she won't be long.

(*We are back with* **WILL** *and* **VIOLA.**)

WILL. You cannot marry him! Not for the Queen herself!

VIOLA. What will you have me do? Marry you instead?

WILL. Yes.

VIOLA. Idiot. It's impossible. I must go to Greenwich today.

WILL. I will go with you.

VIOLA. Wessex will kill you.

WILL. I know how to fight.

VIOLA. Stage fighting. Oh, Will! As Thomas Kent my heart belongs to you but as Viola the river divides us, and I will marry Wessex a week from Saturday.

WILL. No. Now that I have found you I will never be parted from you.

WESSEX. I will wait no longer!

NURSE. My Lord, you cannot enter a young lady's bedchamber.

WESSEX. By heaven, I will drag her down by the Queen's command. Convention be damned, I'm going in!

> (**VIOLA**, *by now almost dressed, has bundled* **WILL**, *his clothes, and the large laundry basket into the bed and has closed the bed-curtains. She positions herself and puts the finishing touches to her dress as* **WESSEX** *enters.*)

NURSE. My Lady, Lord Wessex is here.

WESSEX. Ah! My Lady! Here, in your bedchamber, all alone. What on earth has kept you? We are due in Greenwich in less than an hour. And the Queen waits for no one.

VIOLA. I must look presentable.

WESSEX. The tide waits for no man but I swear it would wait for you! By my heavens, you look good enough to ravish here and now.

> (WESSEX *roughly takes* VIOLA*'s wrist and pulls her to the bed. She resists.*)

VIOLA. Lord Wessex!

WESSEX. I said now!

VIOLA. No!

WESSEX. Now!

> (WESSEX *pulls the bed-curtains open. This reveals* WILL, *who has got himself into a dress and headdress.*)

WILL. Beg your pardon, My Lord.

> (WILL *sets about folding a sheet.*)

WESSEX. Who is this?

VIOLA. My…laundry maid.

WILL. And chaperone. My Lady's country cousin. And we'll be kissing cousins when her purse is open to you.

WESSEX. Do you have many relatives?

VIOLA. None so dear as Cousin…Wilhelmina, My Lord.

WILL/WILHELMINA. You may call me Miss Wilhelmina!

WESSEX. On a more fortuitous occasion, perhaps. Come, Viola, we must go!

WILL/WILHELMINA. *(getting very close to* WESSEX*)* Oh, My Lord, you will not shake me off, she never needed me more. I swear by your breeches you be a handsome gallant, just as she said.

WESSEX. Viola! Come with me.

WILL/WILHELMINA. Wait for me, My Lord.

Scene Two

(Greenwich Palace.)

[MUSIC NO. 26: "VIVAT REGINA – ENTRANCE"]

(The **QUEEN**, *her* **ATTENDANTS**, *and the* **COURT** *assemble.)*

COMPANY. *(sung)*

VIVAT REGINA,

VIVAT REGINA,

VIVAT REGINA,

VIVAT! VIVAT!

VIVAT!!!

WESSEX. Now?

TILNEY. Now, My Lord.

WESSEX. The Queen asks for you. Answer well.

> *(**TILNEY** escorts **VIOLA** through the crowd – this is a formal affair. He leads her to the **QUEEN**. **WESSEX** is left with **WILL** still dressed as Wilhelmina.)*

There is a man behind this pretence.

WILL/WILHELMINA. A man, My Lord?

WESSEX. I am no fool. There was a poet…a theatre poet I heard. Does he come to the house?

WILL/WILHELMINA. A poet?

WESSEX. An insolent penny-a-page rogue, Marlowe. A Christopher Marlowe. Has he been to the house?

WILL/WILHELMINA. Marlowe. Oh yes, he's the one. Lovely doublet, shame about the verse.

WESSEX. The dog!

> *(**TILNEY** presents **VIOLA** to the **QUEEN**.)*

QUEEN. What a smile you have, Mister Tilney. Like a brass plate on a coffin.

TILNEY. Your Majesty. The Lady Viola de Lesseps.

VIOLA. Your Majesty.

QUEEN. Stand up straight, girl. *(examines* **VIOLA***)* I have seen you. You are the one who comes to all the plays… at Whitehall, at Richmond.

VIOLA. Your Majesty.

QUEEN. What do you love so much?

VIOLA. Your Majesty…?

QUEEN. Speak out! I know who I am. Do you love stories of kings and queens? Feats of arms? Or is it courtly love?

VIOLA. I love theatre. To have stories acted for me by a company of fellows is indeed—

QUEEN. They are not acted for you, they are acted for me.

(Obsequious laughter from the **COURT**.*)*

And…?

VIOLA. I love poetry above all.

QUEEN. Above Lord Wessex? My Lord, when you cannot find your wife you had better look for her at the playhouse.

TILNEY. Hardly a place for a young lady of breeding, Your Majesty.

QUEEN. Oh, I am all for the theatre, Mister Tilney. But playwrights teach nothing about love; they make it pretty, they make it comical, or they make it lust. They cannot make it true.

VIOLA. Oh, but they can!

(A gasp from the **COURT**.*)*

TILNEY. Her Majesty is not in the habit of being contradicted.

VIOLA. I mean…Your Majesty, they do not, they have not, but I believe there is one who can.

(Horrified, **WESSEX** *rushes to intervene.)*

WESSEX. Lady Viola is…young in the world. Your Majesty is wise in it. Nature and truth are the very enemies of playacting. I'll wager my fortune.

QUEEN. I thought you were here because you had none. Well, will anyone take Lord Wessex up on his wager? Mister Tilney?

TILNEY. The Lord Chamberlain cannot be seen to gamble, Your Majesty.

QUEEN. Lady Viola, it seems no one will risk this wager.

WILL/WILHELMINA. Fifty pounds.

QUEEN. I hear from somewhere fifty pounds. A very worthy sum on a very worthy question. Can a play show us the very truth and nature of love? I bear witness to the wager, and will be the judge of it as occasion arises.

TILNEY. A conceit of genius, Your Majesty.

*(**TILNEY** leads a scatter of applause.)*

QUEEN. I have not seen anything to settle it yet. So. The fireworks will be soothing after the excitements of Lady Viola's audience. *(intimately, to **WESSEX**)* Have her then, but you are a lordly fool. She has been plucked since I saw her last and not by you. It takes a woman to know it.

WESSEX. *(aside)* Marlowe. I will kill the wretch.

[MUSIC NO. 27: "VIVAT REGINA – EXIT"]

*(**WESSEX** turns to watch the fireworks just beginning. There are gasps from the **CROWD** at each explosion. **WILL**, still in disguise, pulls **VIOLA** aside.)*

WILL. Viola, Viola! I must away to my pages. I will see you at the theatre.

VIOLA. Please, Will, be careful.

WILL. Don't worry, no one will recognise me here.

(**WILL** *turns and immediately bumps into*
MARLOWE.)

MARLOWE. Will! Is there something you haven't told me?

WILL. What are you doing here, Kit?

MARLOWE. I have come incognito.

WILL. What for?

MARLOWE. Call it a truant disposition. Don't you have a
play to write?

WILL. Yes, but I have a commission of the heart. Lady
Viola—

MARLOWE. *(interrupting)* Don't get distracted, Will. God
has given you one face, and you run around with
another, in a dress! Leave deception to those better
suited. Go home and finish your play. You could be
the best of all of us. Besides, what if you get caught?

WILL. And what about you, Kit?

MARLOWE. Don't worry, no one is going to recognise me
here.

(**BURBAGE** *enters.*)

BURBAGE. Marlowe.

MARLOWE. Burbage.

(**WILL** *moves to exit.*)

BURBAGE. Hello, young lady.

(**WILL** *laughs girlishly as he leaves.*)

MARLOWE. What are you doing here, Burbage?

BURBAGE. I have come to give my *Faustus* for Her Majesty
this very evening.

MARLOWE. Your *Faustus*? Burbage, you thief. You already
owe me twenty pounds. My *Massacre at Paris* is
complete, or shall I give the play to Ned Alleyn?

BURBAGE. You have the pages?

MARLOWE. You have the money?

BURBAGE. Tomorrow.

MARLOWE. Then tomorrow you have the pages. When I've had what I am owed for your royal *Faustus*.

BURBAGE. Come, what is money to men like us? Besides, if I need a play I have another waiting, a comedy by Shakespeare.

MARLOWE. *Romeo*? He gave it to Henslowe.

BURBAGE. Never! I gave Shakespeare two sovereigns for *Romeo*!

MARLOWE. You did. But Henslowe rehearses it as we speak.

BURBAGE. Treachery! Traitor and thief.

MARLOWE. Well, I am to Deptford. Tomorrow.

BURBAGE. Won't you stay, Kit, for my performance?

MARLOWE. I refuse to stay and see myself murdered here tonight. Twenty pounds, Burbage. The fee simple! Oh simple!

BURBAGE. Henslowe is rehearsing my play?

MARLOWE. With Alleyn. As we speak.

Scene Three

(The Rose Theatre. Rehearsals.)

NED. Gentlemen, from the top of the scene, with words.

[MUSIC NO. 28: "REHEARSALS"]

(The scene assembles; **NED** *as Mercutio and* **NOL** *as Benvolio have swords and are squared up against* **PETER** *as Tybalt and* **RALPH** *as Petruchio. They too have swords.* **WEBSTER** *reads a script in a corner as* **HENSLOWE** *and* **FENNYMAN** *look on.)*

NOL/BENVOLIO.

By my head, here comes the Capulets.

NED/MERCUTIO.

By my heel, I care not.

PETER/TYBALT.

Follow me close, for I will speak to them.

Gentlemen, good e'en. A word with one of you.

NED/MERCUTIO. *(as* **NED***)* Are you really going to do it like that? *(back in scene)*

And but one word with one of us?

Couple it with something; make it a word and a blow.

(Enter **VIOLA** *as Romeo.)*

PETER/TYBALT.

Well, peace be with you, sir. Here comes my man.

Romeo, thou art a villain.

VIOLA/ROMEO.

I do protest I never injured thee,

But love thee better than thou canst devise

Till thou shalt know the reason of my love;

And so, good Capulet, which name I tender

As dear as my own, be satisfied.

NED/MERCUTIO.

    O calm, dishonourable, vile submission!

    Tybalt, you rat-catcher, will you walk?

PETER/TYBALT.

    I am for you.

        (**TYBALT** *attacks* **MERCUTIO** *as the scene*
        continues.)

VIOLA/ROMEO.

    Gentle Mercutio, put thy rapier up.

    Draw, Benvolio; beat down their weapons.

    Gentlemen, for shame! forbear this outrage!

    Tybalt, Mercutio, the Prince expressly hath forbid…

    Hold, Tybalt! Good Mercutio!

        (**TYBALT** *stabs* **MERCUTIO.**)

RALPH/PETRUCHIO.

    Away, Tybalt!

        (**TYBALT** *runs offstage.*)

NOL/BENVOLIO.

    What, art thou hurt?

NED/MERCUTIO.

    Ay, ay, a scratch. Marry 'tis enough.

    Ask for me tomorrow, and you shall find me a grave
        man.

        (**BURBAGE** *arrives with two* **HEAVIES.**)

BURBAGE. I'll see you hanged, Henslowe! I have come for
my play, you scoundrels. Give me that manuscript.

        (**BURBAGE** *sees* **WILL** *with the manuscript, draws*
        his rapier on him, and the **HEAVIES** *advance.*)

NED. How dare you, sir? No one interrupts my rehearsals.

BURBAGE. Your rehearsals?

NED. Ignore him, Master Kent – continue!

BURBAGE. Give me that manuscript.

(**WILL** *sprints to avoid* **BURBAGE** *and his* **HEAVIES**.)

VIOLA/KENT. Quick, Will. Careful, Will. Don't let him get it.

HEAVY 1. Fetch him off!

HEAVY 2. Have at thee, boy!

NED. Out of my rehearsals, you talentless dog. I will chop you to pieces.

WILL. *(throwing the manuscript to* **HENSLOWE***)* Henslowe, catch!

BURBAGE. Upstairs. Get that manuscript.

NED. Henslowe. Do something…

HENSLOWE. I am doing something.

NED. Turn thy back and run.

SAM. Down here. Down here.

BURBAGE. Stop him. Get it!

HENSLOWE. Catch it, Master Kent.

> (**HENSLOWE** *throws the manuscript toward* **VIOLA**, *exactly where* **WEBSTER** *is reading his script.* **VIOLA** *and* **WEBSTER** *both reach up to catch it, and* **VIOLA** *ends up with Webster's script, which begins to be tossed around.* **WEBSTER**, *unalarmed, continues to read, now* Romeo and Juliet.*)

NED. I've had enough of you, you ridiculous cur. I will tear your liver out!

BURBAGE. I'll not leave here till I have it. Give me that manuscript!

> (**NED** *and* **BURBAGE** *go into a full-scale sword fight while the swapped manuscript is pursued around the stage.*)

WILL. Master Kent, the manuscript. Master Kent.

HENSLOWE. Why don't you leave off fighting till you're Tamburlaine, Burbage?

VIOLA/KENT. Will!

> *(In the tussle, Burbage's* **HEAVY** *slams* **WILL** *and* **NOL***'s heads together and gets the swapped manuscript.* **BURBAGE** *has incapacitated* **NED***, who is lying at Burbage's sword point.)*

HEAVY 1. *(giving* **BURBAGE** *the swapped manuscript)* Mister Burbage.

BURBAGE. Your swordsmanship's a little rusty, Alleyn. *(holding the swapped manuscript)* Thank you, Master Shakespeare. The play's the thing! Rehearsals will begin with my men, Monday at the Curtain.

> *(***BURBAGE** *and his* **HEAVIES** *leave.)*

HENSLOWE. Let's not panic, we'll think of something.

FENNYMAN. You're an idiot. I was just starting to enjoy myself. Henslowe, there's the small matter of sixteen pounds, five shillings and ninepence…

WEBSTER. *(reciting from the manuscript he has been reading)* "That which we call a rose

By any other name would smell as sweet…"

HENSLOWE. What's that?

WEBSTER. Juliet.

WILL. This is my play.

WEBSTER. Yeah…I was learning that.

VIOLA/KENT. You swapped it?

WEBSTER. Yeah, I swapped it for *Gammer Gurton's Needle.*

WILL. Mister Henslowe, the manuscript.

HENSLOWE. We are saved!

FENNYMAN. Gentlemen. A famous victory! We have the manuscript.

> *(Cheers.)*

A cause for celebration.

> *[MUSIC NO. 29: "INTO THE TAVERN"]*

> (**WILL** *pulls* **VIOLA** *aside.*)

WILL. Viola. Are you all right?

VIOLA. Oh, Will. I have never been happier.

WILL. Come, let's get you home.

VIOLA. No, I want to have a drink with the lads.

WILL. I really don't think that's a good idea.

VIOLA. And then I'm gonna drink you under the table.

> (*Thinking themselves concealed,* **VIOLA** *and* **WILL** *kiss passionately…but* **WEBSTER** *is watching.*)

Scene Four

(Tavern/Brothel. The **ACTORS** *celebrate with* **MOLLY** *and* **KATE,** *tavern whores, as* **MUSICIANS** *play.)*

FENNYMAN. Gentlemen, actors, swordsmen. You are welcome. *(to* **MUSICIANS***)* Shut it. *(to* **ACTORS***)* Gentlemen! The kegs and legs, open and on me. Everything, and I mean everything, is on the house.

(Cheers.)

MOLLY. Brace yourself, Kate.

FENNYMAN. Sam, I think it is time you sampled the delights of a real, living, breathing lady.

MOLLY. You send that little one up here to me.

FENNYMAN. Off you go.

*(***SAM*** heads towards* **MOLLY.***)*

VIOLA/KENT. I thought this was a tavern.

WILL. It is also a tavern.

VIOLA/KENT. This is a house of ill repute.

WILL. But of good reputation. Come, there's no harm in drink.

*(***KATE*** straddles* **WILL.***)*

KATE. I remember you! The poet.

WILL. Must have been someone else. Thomas Dekker, perchance?

KATE. No, I remember – you have a silver tongue.

VIOLA/KENT. Excuse me, we are trying to have a civilised conversation.

KATE. *(taking an interest in* **KENT***)* Now here's a pretty one!

VIOLA/KENT. Excuse me, darling, I'm trying to have a drink.

FENNYMAN. Master Kent! Will you not dip your wick, sir?

VIOLA/KENT. My wick?

WILL. Mister Fennyman! We were in fact discussing your great love of the theatre, and Master Kent suggested you should have a part in the play.

FENNYMAN. Me?!

WILL. I am writing an Apothecary, a small but vital role.

FENNYMAN. By heaven I thank you. I will play...no, no, I will be your Apothecary. I am to be in the play!

KATE. What's this play about then?

RALPH. Well, there's this nurse...

> (**SAM** *reappears with* **MOLLY** – *a huge smile on his face.*)

NOL. Oy, oy! He's back.

MOLLY. It was very quick.

SAM. It was <u>very</u> quick. But I liked it.

> (*Cheers.*)

FENNYMAN. Come, Sam, take some ale. Mister Henslowe, Mister Shakespeare has given me the part of the Apothecary.

HENSLOWE. The Apothecary? What about the shipwreck? How does it end, Will?

WILL. By God, I wish I knew.

HENSLOWE. I paid for pirates, clowns, and a happy end. If I don't get reconciliations and a jig I will send you back to Stratford...to your wife!!

VIOLA/KENT. Wife?!

WILL. Erm...

HENSLOWE. And the twins!

WILL. (*to* **VIOLA**) I can explain. I was only eighteen. My marriage is long dead and buried in Stratford. Everything I am is here in London. With you.

VIOLA/KENT. *(distraught)* I have risked everything and you have done nothing but lie.

WILL. No. I love you. I love you more than all writing. I love you more than life itself.

VIOLA/KENT. It's over, Will. I can never see you again.

> *(**VIOLA** runs out, evading **WILL**, as **PETER** runs in.)*

PETER. Will! Mister Henslowe! Gentlemen! A black day for us all! There is news come up river from Deptford. Marlowe is dead. Stabbed! Stabbed to death in a tavern in Deptford. Kit Marlowe is dead.

WILL. What have I done?

NED. He was the first man among us.

> *[MUSIC NO. 30: "MARLOWE'S DEATH"]*

A great light has gone out.

WILL. Kit. Kit…

MUSICIANS. *(sung)*

BUT THY ETERNAL SUMMER SHALL NOT FADE

NOR LOSE POSSESSION OF,

NOR LOSE THAT FAIR THOU OW'ST,

NOR SHALL DEATH BRAG THOU WAND'REST IN HIS SHADE.

WILL. Wessex.

Scene Five

(Viola's bedroom. **VIOLA** *is in bed, sobbing.*
NURSE *enters.)*

NURSE. My Lady! My Lady, My Lady, what is the matter?

VIOLA. Just leave me, Nursey.

WESSEX. *(offstage)* Viola!

NURSE. Lord Wessex is here.

VIOLA. Tell him I'm asleep, tell him anything, just make him go away.

*(***WESSEX*** bursts in.)*

WESSEX. Let me through!

NURSE. No! Sir…I'm sorry, Ma'am.

*(***WESSEX*** stands before* **VIOLA**, *smouldering with drink-fuelled lust.)*

WESSEX. Ah my sad, sweet angel.

VIOLA. What is the meaning of this?!

WESSEX. Here you are. Ready. Undone. I have been minded, your father away, that as he is paying good money for me that I should at least allow you the privilege of caveat emptor. Buyer beware. One would hate you to be disappointed on the wedding night if you found the purchase not in good working order. *(to* **NURSE***)* Leave us, Nursey. A pint of Madeira when I call. *(to* **VIOLA***)* I see you have been crying. I understand, of course. I never met the poor fellow but once in your house. But you have my commiserations.

VIOLA. "Poor fellow"?

WESSEX. Oh! Dear God, I did not think it would be me to tell you! A great loss to theatre, to playwriting, dancing, and so forth.

VIOLA. I don't understand.

WESSEX. Your playwright is dead.

VIOLA. Dead?!

WESSEX. Dead!

VIOLA. Impossible.

WESSEX. Stabbed to death this very night, in a tavern – I heard.

> (**VIOLA** *faints.* **WESSEX** *starts to unbutton himself.*)

Exquisitely sensitive.

> (*A crack of thunder.*)

Nice weather for it. Nursey, I'll have that Madeira!

WILL. *(from offstage)* Viola!

WESSEX. *(irritated at the interruption)* Odd's fish!

> (**WILL** *arrives bedraggled, haunted, otherworldly. He comes into the room.* **WESSEX** *gasps in horror.*)

Marlowe! Avaunt and quit my sight, thou phantom!

WILL. *(seeing* **VIOLA** *prostrate)* Viola! No.

WESSEX. Spare me, for the love of God!

> (**WESSEX** *flees.*)

WILL. Oh, my love. If there be no breath on your lips let the worms have me too.

> (**WILL** *kisses* **VIOLA**. *She stirs.*)

VIOLA. He said you were dead.

WILL. No, I am alive.

VIOLA. You were stabbed in a tavern?

WILL. No, no, it's worse…Marlowe. Unwittingly I led him to his death. I would exchange all my plays to come for all his that will never be written, do you understand? Kit is dead. He was the brightest light of us all. He was my friend and I led him to his death. And all of my stuff is just worthless now, just scribblings in the wind. *(tears some pages into pieces)* I'll never write again. Oh God, oh God, Kit, Kit.

VIOLA. Oh, my darling, this is madness. Marlowe is dead, but you must live. You must write. Would Kit have wanted this? *(pieces fragments together and reads)*

Wilt thou be gone? It is not yet near day.
It was the nightingale, and not the lark,
That pierced the fearful hollow of thine ear.
Nightly she sings on yon pomegranate tree.
Believe me, love, it was the nightingale.

What is this?

WILL. Nothing, just some new scene I wrote you.

VIOLA. More false words?

WILL. My love was no lie. It needs no wife from Stratford to tell you I could never marry the daughter of Robert de Lesseps. It is the scene after they have first made love.

[MUSIC NO. 31: "R&J PLOT"]

It was the lark, the herald of the morn;
No nightingale. Look, love, what envious streaks
Do lace the severing clouds in yonder East.
Night's candles are burnt out, and jocund day
Stands tiptoe on the misty mountain tops.
I must be gone and live, or stay and die.

(Gradually the text brings **VIOLA** *and* **WILL** *together.)*

VIOLA.

Yond light is not daylight; I know it, I.
It is some meteor that the sun exhales
To be to thee this night a torchbearer...

WILL.

I have more care to stay than will to go.
Come, death, and welcome! Juliet wills it so.

VIOLA. It is beautiful. All my previous passions were vanity. I did not truly love you till now. And then...?

WILL. For killing Juliet's kinsman Tybalt, the one who
    killed Romeo's friend Mercutio, Romeo is banished
    from Verona. But the Friar who married Romeo and
    Juliet...

Scene Six

(The Rose Theatre. WILL *is now talking to the* COMPANY.*)*

WILL. …gives Juliet a potion to drink. It is a secret potion. It makes her seeming dead. She is placed in the tomb of the Capulets. She will awake to life and love when Romeo comes to her side again.

RALPH. Excellent.

[END MUSIC NO. 31]

WILL. I have not said all. By malign fate, the message goes astray which would tell Romeo of the Friar's plan. He hears only that Juliet is dead. And with this he goes to the Apothecary.

FENNYMAN. That's me.

WILL. Romeo buys a deadly poison then enters the tomb to bid farewell to his Juliet who lies cold as stone. He drinks the poison. He dies by her side. Juliet wakes and she sees her Romeo lying there beside her. And so Juliet takes his dagger and with it she kills herself.

HENSLOWE. Well, that will have them rolling in the aisles.

WILL. It is complete.

*(*WILL *hands the complete manuscript to* HENSLOWE.*)*

FENNYMAN. Sad and wonderful. I have at home a blue velvet cap. I have seen an apothecary with a cap just so. Have I got time to go and get it?

WILL. I don't think it matters about the cap.

(But FENNYMAN *is gone.* WESSEX *enters.)*

WESSEX. Out of my way.

HENSLOWE. My Lord Wessex!

WESSEX. You! Who are you? You're not Marlowe!

HENSLOWE. I didn't know you were a patron of the arts. Get him a chair, someone.

WESSEX. *(to* **WILL***)* You inconsequential coward. This time I will cut you to pieces.

*(***BURBAGE** *enters.)*

BURBAGE. Shakespeare! You owe me a play.

WESSEX. Shakespeare!?

*(***WILL** *and* **WESSEX** *fight. The fight culminates in* **WILL** *stabbing* **WESSEX** *with a dagger, much to the* **COMPANY***'s horror.)*

WESSEX. *(realizing it is a theatrical prop, draws his own)* This is a dagger.

*(***WILL** *and* **WESSEX** *continue to fight.)*

WILL. This is the murderer of Kit Marlowe!

*(***WILL** *is about to deal the fatal blow…)*

EVERYONE. No!!

WESSEX. I rejoiced at his death because I thought it was yours. That is all I know of Marlowe.

NED. It's true, Will. It was a tavern brawl. Marlowe attacked – got his own knife in his eye. A quarrel about the bill.

HENSLOWE. The bill! Oh, vanity, vanity.

NED. Not the billing. The <u>bill</u>.

*(***TILNEY** *enters with* **WEBSTER***.)*

TILNEY. Enough of this play-acting. This theatre is closed.

HENSLOWE. Mister Tilney. What is this?

TILNEY. The theatre. A pit of sedition, filth, and treachery. I'd have them all ploughed into the ground and covered over with lime— *(sees* **WESSEX** *and bows)* My Lord Wessex.

WESSEX. Carry on, Tilney.

TILNEY. Under the seal of the Lord Chamberlain, the Rose Theatre is closed for public indecency.

HENSLOWE. Admittedly we are under-rehearsed, but is this really a <u>moral</u> issue?

TILNEY. For the displaying of a female on the public stage.

> (**TILNEY** *grabs* **SAM** *and lifts up his skirt.*)

WEBSTER. Not him. Her.

> (**WEBSTER** *advances on* **VIOLA**.)

TILNEY. Him?!

HENSLOWE. Master Kent's a woman?!

TILNEY. Really?

WEBSTER. Look.

> (**WEBSTER** *whips off* **VIOLA**'s *hat and moustache.*)

TILNEY. My Lady de Lesseps!

HENSLOWE. Viola de Lesseps?

WESSEX. Viola! Good God. Here. Dressed as a common actor. Tilney, do your duty.

TILNEY. Henslowe!

HENSLOWE. I am amazed. I knew nothing of this.

VIOLA. Nobody knew.

WEBSTER. *(points to* WILL*)* He did. I saw him kissing her bubbies.

TILNEY. Kissing her where?!

WEBSTER. In the wardrobe. Him.

TILNEY. Let me be straight with you. Her Majesty is only too willing to bid these dens of vice farewell. Henslowe, you will never play again. The Rose Theatre is closed.

> (**TILNEY** *storms off.*)

WESSEX. *(to* WILL*)* I came to have your life. But it is not worth the taking. Viola, come with me.

VIOLA. I am so sorry, Mister Henslowe, Mister Alleyn, Sam, Mister Wabash. I just wanted to be an actor.

WABASH. Y-y-y-y-y-y-y-you w-w-were w-w-w-w-wonderful.

WILL. Wait! Take this and remember me.

>*(**WILL** takes the manuscript and gives it to*
>***VIOLA**.)*

WESSEX. Viola!

>*(**VIOLA** leaves with **WESSEX**.)*

WEBSTER. *(to **WILL**)* Should've let me play Ethel then,
shouldn't ya.

>*(**WEBSTER** exits. **FENNYMAN** arrives in his blue*
>*cap.)*

FENNYMAN. Everything all right?

HENSLOWE. Closed before we opened. Let's pack
everything up.

BURBAGE. Hold!

HENSLOWE. Oh God!

BURBAGE. Enemies. Brothers. Lend me your ears. We
may indeed be rivals in art but we are jointly despised
as vagrants, tinkers, peddlers of bombast. Which
in my case might be true. But— (*to* **MUSICIANS**)
Gentlemen...

>*(The **MUSICIANS** start to play:)*

>*[MUSIC NO. 32: "BURBAGE"]*

...my father James Burbage had the first licence
to form a company of players and he drew from
all the poets of the age. Their fame will be our
fame. So let them all know, we are men of parts.
We are a fraternity, and we will be a profession.
Will Shakespeare has a play. I have a theatre. To be
frank the posters are already posted. Damn the Lord
Chamberlain. The Curtain is yours.

HENSLOWE. There is no time to be lost. We will play *Romeo*
this Saturday at the Curtain.

BURBAGE. But who will be our Romeo?

HENSLOWE. Will. You already know the part.

Scene Seven

[MUSIC NO. 33: "WEDDING"]

(The wedding of WESSEX *and* VIOLA *as a dumb-show masque to beautiful music.* VIOLA *appears in a wedding dress.* DE LESSEPS *takes her hand and leads the bride to* WESSEX. NURSE *looks on. The marriage ceremony takes place in the grand language of court theatre, contrasting with the speed and fluency of Shakespeare's rough playhouse world.* VIOLA *is solemn, broken-hearted, as she consigns herself to a lifetime of misery. The bride and groom are married and finally kiss in a shaft of white light.)*

COMPANY. *(sung)*

ALLELUIA ALLELUIA

ALLELUIA

ALLELUIA ALLELUIA

ALLELUIA

ALLELUIA ALLELUIA

ALLELUIA

Scene Eight

(A room in De Lesseps Hall. DE LESSEPS is at a desk. WESSEX is in attendance. NURSE looks on.)

DE LESSEPS. Lord Wessex, son-in-law. I trust you are all set.

WESSEX. Indeed, sir, we are for Virginia this afternoon. All is as planned. Except for the matter of the money.

DE LESSEPS. By these drafts in my hand you gain five thousand pounds.

WESSEX. Thank you, but would you oblige me fifty or so in gold? To settle my accounts at dockside. *(shouts offstage)* Come, Viola. We must away.

> *(**DE LESSEPS** opens the desk and unlocks the gold.)*

NURSE. *(to **WESSEX**)* Please, sir, may I ask of you that you be good to her, sir?

WESSEX. Of course.

NURSE. Treat her kindly, sir.

WESSEX. I will.

NURSE. You are a good man, sir.

WESSEX. Thank you.

NURSE. I feel it in my heart. A very good man, sir.

WESSEX. Please let go of my arm. There's a good Nursey.

NURSE. God bless you, sir. And another thing, sir.

WESSEX. Let it wait, woman. We must away. Come, Viola. The tide waits for no man.

> *(**WESSEX** goes to fetch **VIOLA**, as **NURSE** opens up a playbill she has hidden.)*

She's gone!

> *[MUSIC NO. 34: "FENNYMAN"]*

NURSE. Gone, sir?

DE LESSEPS. Gone?

NURSE. *(aside)* Oh yes, she has gone.

DE LESSEPS. Gone where?

NURSE. I don't know, sir.

> (WESSEX *returns, sees the playbill, and takes it from* NURSE.)

WESSEX. What is this?

> "By permission of Mr Burbage
> A Hugh Fennyman production
> of Mister Henslowe's presentation of
> The Admiral's Men in performance of
> The Excellent and Lamentable Tragedy of
> *Romeo and Juliet*
> Featuring Mister Fennyman as the Apothecary
> at the Curtain Theatre!"

Scene Nine

(The Curtain Theatre, backstage. **MUSICIANS**
play. **FENNYMAN** *practises his lines.)*

FENNYMAN/APOTHECARY.

Such mortal drugs I have; but Mantua's law
Is death to any he that utters them.

(to **MUSICIANS***)* Shut it!!! *(back to practising)* Then him.
Then me.

(The stage erupts with **ACTORS***.)*

HENSLOWE. Beginners to the stage, please. This is your
two-minute call.

NED. Good luck, gentlemen. Break a leg!

HENSLOWE. Cheer up, Will. It's a full house. Two
thousand people.

*(***SAM** *is gargling from a beaker.)*

WILL. Are you okay, Sam? The whole thing is hopeless.

HENSLOWE. At least it's stopped raining.

WILL. We've hardly rehearsed and half the company
have no idea what their lines are. We'll be hanged,
Henslowe.

HENSLOWE. Peace, Will. It will all turn out fine in the end.
Beginners to the stage – quickly, quickly. Ah, Mister
Wabash, ready for your big moment?

WABASH. Two households both alike in d-d-d-d-d-d-
dignity…

WILL. We are lost.

HENSLOWE. No, it will turn out well.

WILL. How will it turn out well?

HENSLOWE. I don't know. It's a mystery.

WILL. Good luck, Sam.

>   (**SAM** *makes a long, deep growling sound.*)
> Sam?!?

HENSLOWE. All those expectant faces. Expecting a man with a dog. Never mind, eh? Good luck everybody.

>   (*The* **COMPANY** *ritually touches hands.*)

COMPANY. One, two, three...to silence.

HENSLOWE. Off we go.

WILL. Good luck, Mister Wabash.

WABASH. Break a leg yourself, W...W...W...Will.

HENSLOWE. I think he'll be fine. Music, trumpets!

>   (*Fanfare.*)
>   [MUSIC NO. 35: "R&J PROLOGUE"]

And...the Chorus. Mister Wabash, on you go.

>   (*The scene flips front, facing the audience.*
>   **WABASH** *is agonisingly alone on stage. An awful pause.*)

WABASH. T-t-t-t-t-t- (*stops and decides to have another go*) T-t-t-t-t-t t-t-t-t-t-t-t-t-twooooo...h-h-households b-both alike in d-d-d-ignity. (*suddenly finds his voice and is wonderfully fluent*)

In fair Verona, where we lay our scene,
From ancient grudge break to new mutiny,
Where civil blood makes civil hands unclean.
From forth the fatal loins of these two foes
A pair of star-crossed lovers take their life;
Whose misadventured piteous overthrows
Doth with their death bury their parents' strife...

>   [MUSIC NO. 36: "R&J PROLOGUE END"]
>   (*The scene flips to backstage.*)

HENSLOWE. It's a mystery, Mister Shakespeare. A mystery.

>   (**WABASH** *collapses, overcome.*)

WILL. Wonderful!

WABASH. Was it any g-g-g-g-g-g-good?

HENSLOWE. Nol and Adam! On you go.

> *[MUSIC NO. 37: "R&J – UNDERSCORE"]*
>
> (Romeo and Juliet *begins. In the following sequence, the text on the left is happening "backstage" in the foreground, and the text on the right is happening "onstage" in the background.*)

NOL/SAMPSON. Gregory, on my word, we'll not carry coals.

ADAM/GREGORY. No, for then we should be colliers.

SAM. *(growls)* Arghhhh. Garrgh.

NOL/SAMPSON. A dog of the house of Montague moves me.

WILL. Sam?

ADAM/GREGORY. Draw thy tool! Here comes two of their house. I will bite my thumb at them.

SAM. Master Shakespeare. My voice!

WILL. Sam! Do me a speech. Do me a line! A word!

ABRAHAM. Do you bite your thumb at us, sir?

SAM. *(deep bass)* Romeo, Romeo!

ADAM/GREGORY. No. Do you quarrel, sir?

ABRAHAM. Quarrel, sir? No, sir.

WILL. He can't say a word. We are lost. Again.

NOL/SAMPSON. Draw, if you be men. Gregory, remember thy swashing blow.

SAM. Wherefore art thou Romeo?

HENSLOWE. No one will notice.

NED/MERCUTIO. Part, fools! Put up your swords. You know not what you do.

WILL. What will we do?

HENSLOWE. Juliet doesn't come on for twenty pages. Give him cider vinegar and honey.

PETER. He's been gargling cider vinegar all day, sir.

HENSLOWE. Go and rest your voice, boy. It will be all right.

WILL. How can it possibly be all right?

> **ADAM/BENVOLIO.** Good morrow, cousin.

PETER. Will, your cue!

(**WILL** *goes onstage.*)

> **WILL/ROMEO.** Is the day so young?

(*Enter* **BURBAGE.**)

BURBAGE. Is everything all right?

HENSLOWE. We have no Juliet.

BURBAGE. What do you mean, no Juliet?

HENSLOWE. He's lost his voice.

> **ADAM/BENVOLIO.** But new struck nine.

BURBAGE. Lost his voice?

HENSLOWE. Yes, but it will all be all right.

BURBAGE. How will it be all right?

> **WILL/ROMEO.** Ay me! Sad hours seem long.

HENSLOWE. I don't know. It's a mystery.

BURBAGE. Does anyone else know the part?

COMPANY. No.

WEBSTER. I do! "Oh Romeo, Romeo, wherefore art thou Romeo?"

BURBAGE. This is a disaster!

(Enter **VIOLA.***)*

HENSLOWE. No women backstage!

VIOLA. It's me.

HENSLOWE. Who are you?

VIOLA. Thomas Kent.

HENSLOWE. What are you doing here?

VIOLA. Since I cannot watch the play, please let me hear it from backstage.

HENSLOWE. There will be no play; we do not have a Juliet.

[MUSIC NO. 38: "R&J SCENE LINK"]

VIOLA. What happened to Sam?

HENSLOWE. We are lost, his voice has just broken, he can't get a word out.

ADAM/BENVOLIO. What sadness lengthens Romeo's hours?

WILL/ROMEO. Not having that which having makes them short.

ADAM/BENVOLIO. In love?

WILL/ROMEO. Out...

ADAM/BENVOLIO. Of love?

Examine other beauties, your lady's love against some other maid. That I will show you shining at this feast.

WILL/ROMEO. I'll go along, no such sight to be shown, but to rejoice in splendour of my own.

NED. That's it, we'll have to cancel the show.

FENNYMAN. Do you realise how long it's taken me to learn this bloody part?

(**FENNYMAN** *beats* **SAM** *with his blue cap. The* **COMPANY** *set the next scene, in Juliet's bedchamber.* **WILL** *comes backstage.*)

WILL. Viola, is this a dream? You have come back to me.

VIOLA. I am married, Will. I sail this afternoon for Virginia.

WILL. Without me?!?

VIOLA. Will. No. These are our last stolen moments. Do not spoil them.

WILL. I will never be parted from you.

ADAM. Will. The curtain!

(**WILL** *opens the curtain to allow* **ROBIN** *and* **RALPH** *onstage to play their scene. Backstage,* **VIOLA** *speaks along with the scene.*)

VIOLA.
Nurse, where's my
daughter? Call her forth
to me.

ROBIN/LADY CAPULET.
Nurse, where's my
daughter? Call her forth
to me.

RALPH/NURSE.

Now, by my maidenhead
at twelve year old, I bade
her come. What, lamb!
What ladybird!

Now, by my maidenhead
at twelve year old, I bade
her come. What, lamb!
What ladybird!

NED. This is Sam's entrance.

VIOLA. God forbid, where's
this girl? What, Juliet!

God forbid, where's
this girl? What, Juliet!
(pause, repeats) What,
Juliet?

SAM. *(makes a huge noise)*
Gaaarrgh!

BURBAGE. He can't go on,
we must stop the show.

HENSLOWE. I will make the
announcement.

VIOLA.
What, Juliet?
(alone) How now? Who
calls?

RALPH/NURSE.
What, Juliet?

(The **COMPANY** *all
hear* **VIOLA** *say this
final line.)*

Your mother calls.

NED. Do you know this?

VIOLA. Every word.

NED. Well. On.

*(An agonising pause
onstage.)*

VIOLA. I can't go on. It's against the law!

HENSLOWE. We'll be hanged if we put a woman on the stage!

RALPH/NURSE. Your mother calls.

NED. There are two thousand people out there who've paid sixpence a ticket.

BURBAGE. We'll be hanged whatever we do.

NED. On!

VIOLA. No, please, no! I can't possibly.

NED. You'll be marvellous.

RALPH/NURSE. Your mother calls!

(VIOLA is pushed onto the stage.)

[MUSIC NO. 39: "VIOLA ONSTAGE"]

(The whole COMPANY creep to where they can see what is happening onstage.)

VIOLA/JULIET. Madam, I am here. What is your will?

ROBIN/LADY CAPULET. Thou knowst my daughter's of a pretty age.

RALPH/NURSE. F…f…faith, I can tell her age unto an hour.

ROBIN/LADY CAPULET. She's not fourteen. Tell me, daughter Juliet, how stands your disposition to be married?

VIOLA/JULIET. It is an honour that I dream not of.

RALPH/NURSE. An honour? Were not I thine only nurse, I would say thou hadst suck'd wisdom from thy teat.

ROBIN/LADY CAPULET. Well, think of marriage now; Speak briefly, can you like of Paris' love?

VIOLA/JULIET. I'll look to like, if looking liking move; but no more deep will I endart mine eye Than your consent gives strength to make it fly.

RALPH/NURSE. Susan and she – God rest all Christian souls! –

HENSLOWE. A mystery. I told you it would be all right.

– were of an age. Well, Susan is with God; She was too good for me.

WABASH. She is w…w… wonderful.

COMPANY. Shhhh!!!

(End of "onstage" and "backstage" overlapping. Enter **TILNEY** *backstage as scene continues in dumb-show onstage.)*

TILNEY. By the power given to me by her Royal Majesty—

COMPANY. Shhhh!!!

TILNEY. I order you to stop this show.

HENSLOWE. Quiet!

TILNEY. Not even you, Mister Henslowe, can deny that *that* is a female on the public stage. Nothing will stop me this time.

> *(The* **COMPANY** *surround* **TILNEY**.*)*

Unhand me, you dogs! In the name of Her Majesty!

> *(***TILNEY*** *is pushed down a trap.)*

WEBSTER. *(to* **TILNEY***)* That'll teach you – should have paid me!

> *(***WESSEX*** *enters.)*

WESSEX. You artless peasants! That is my wife! You curs.

COMPANY. Shhhh!!!

HENSLOWE. Oh God!

WESSEX. I will be the master of what is mine own.

COMPANY. Shhhh!!!

WESSEX. *(drawing his dagger)* This time I spare no quarter, Mister Shakespeare.

> *(The* **DOG** *bounds onstage and jumps up onto* **WESSEX***, pushing him over.)*

HENSLOWE. Put him down with Tilney.

WESSEX. Unhand me!

> *(***WILL*** *grabs the dagger as the* **COMPANY** *force* **WESSEX** *into the trap. Curtains open to reveal the onstage scene.)*

RALPH/NURSE.
   …Lady, such a man
   As all the world – why, he's a man of wax.

ROBIN/LADY CAPULET.
   Verona's summer hath not such a flower.

RALPH/NURSE.
   Nay, he's a flower, in faith – a very flower.

ADAM/SERVINGMAN.
   Madam, the guests are come.

ROBIN/LADY CAPULET.

We follow thee. Juliet, the county stays.

RALPH/NURSE.

Go, girl, seek happy nights to happy days.

(**VIOLA, ROBIN,** *and* **RALPH** *come backstage.*)

VIOLA. I did it, Will. I am a player. I am one of you.

[MUSIC NO. 40: "WILT THOU BE GONE?"]

(*The scene flips with* **VIOLA** *and* **WILL** *onstage together.*)

VIOLA/JULIET.

Wilt thou be gone? It is not yet near day.

It was the nightingale, and not the lark,

That pierced the fearful hollow of thine ear.

Nightly she sings on yon pomegranate tree.

Believe me, love, it was the nightingale.

(**JULIET** *goes to the balcony.*)

WILL/ROMEO.

It was the lark, the herald of the morn;

No nightingale. Look, love, what envious streaks

Do lace the severing clouds in yonder East.

Night's candles are burnt out, and jocund day

Stands tiptoe on the misty mountain tops.

I must be gone and live, or stay and die.

VIOLA/JULIET.

Yond light is not daylight; I know it, I.

It is some meteor that the sun exhales

To be to thee this night a torchbearer

And light thee on thy way to Mantua.

Therefore stay yet; thou need'st not be gone.

WILL/ROMEO.

Let me be ta'en, let me be put to death.

I am content, so thou wilt have it so.

I'll say yon grey is not the morning's eye;
'Tis but the pale reflex of Cynthia's brow.
Nor that is not the lark whose notes do beat
The vaulty heaven so high above our heads.
I have more care to stay than will to go.
Come, death, and welcome! Juliet wills it so.

VIOLA/JULIET.

O, think'st thou we shall ever meet again?

WILL/ROMEO.

I doubt it not; and all these woes shall serve
For sweet discourses in our times to come.

VIOLA/JULIET.

O God, I have an ill-divining soul!
Methinks I see thee now, thou art so low
As one dead in the bottom of a tomb.
Either my eyesight fails, or thou look'st pale.

WILL/ROMEO.

And trust me, love, in my eye so do you.
Dry sorrow drinks our blood. Adieu, adieu!

(The scene flips to backstage.)

HENSLOWE. *(to* **COMPANY***)* Set the table for the Capulet wedding.

FENNYMAN. *(still practising)* Such mortal drugs I have...

[MUSIC NO. 41: "THE KISS"]

WILL. *(to* **VIOLA***)* Come with me...We will leave now.

VIOLA. But the play?

WILL. Forget the play. There is no time.

VIOLA. But where would we go?

WILL. Anywhere.

VIOLA. And leave London? Perhaps I could be poor, Will, but you could never live without the theatre. You

are a dead man without words, and I would be your
murderer.

WILL. No.

VIOLA. If my love means you will write no more, you will
break my heart and my murderer be. Maybe our love
will last twenty years, till we are old and grey. Your
words will be immortal. I cannot be the woman who
denies the whole world William Shakespeare.

WILL. I would not be William Shakespeare for the world if
I could be with you.

VIOLA. Will, on this stage I have been free and I will ever
thank you for it. I will go to Virginia. To grow old and
wise.

WILL. You will never age for me, nor fade, nor die.

VIOLA. Nor you for me.

>   (**WILL** *and* **VIOLA** *kiss.*)

Write me well.

>   (*A flurry of backstage activity.*)

HENSLOWE. A hit. A palpable hit!

NED. The tomb for the final scene.

BURBAGE. We may be closed down – but this is a special
day for the theatre. You will go down with the very
greats. Greene, Kyd, Henry Chettle.

NED. Come, My Lady, we have no time to lose.

>   (*The tomb is set up.*)

Gentlemen.

>   (**EVERYONE** *is still.*)

The final scene.

>   *[MUSIC NO. 42: "JULIET'S TOMB"]*

>   *The scene flips.* **ROMEO** *and* **JULIET** *are alone in
>   the tomb.*)

WILL/ROMEO.

> For here lies Juliet, and her beauty makes
> This vault a feasting presence full of light.
> O, here will I set up my everlasting rest,
> And shake the yoke of inauspicious stars
> From this world-wearied flesh. Eyes, look your last!
> Arms, take your last embrace! and lips, O you
> The doors of breath, seal with a righteous kiss
> A dateless bargain to engrossing death!

> > (ROMEO *kisses* JULIET.)

> Here's to my love! *(drinks)* O true apothecary!
> Thy drugs are quick. Thus with a kiss I die.

> > (JULIET *rouses.*)

VIOLA/JULIET.

> Where is my Romeo?
> What's here? A cup, closed in my true love's hand?
> Poison, I see, hath been his timeless end:
> O churl! Drunk all, and left no friendly drop
> To help me after? I will kiss thy lips.
> Haply some poison yet doth hang on them,
> To make me die with a restorative.

> > (JULIET *kisses* ROMEO. *Now everyone backstage*
> > *is straining to watch the scene.*)

> Thy lips are warm!
> Then I'll be brief. O happy dagger!
> This is thy sheath; there rust, and let me die.

> > (JULIET *stabs herself and falls. Silence. The*
> > *tableau of the dead lovers on the floor. The impact*
> > *of the play is palpable. Suddenly, there is a*
> > *banging beneath and* TILNEY *bursts out through*
> > *the top of the tomb. The* COMPANY *emerges from*
> > *backstage.*)

TILNEY. In the name of Her Majesty, I arrest you all!

WEBSTER. Arrest who?

TILNEY. Everybody! Burbage's Men, Henslowe's Men, the whole of English Theatre – every one of you ne'er-do-wells who stands in contempt of the authority invested in me by Her Majesty.

BURBAGE. Contempt? You closed the Rose. What charge do you lay against the Curtain?

TILNEY. That woman is a woman!

NED. A woman?!

TILNEY. Yes. So in the name of Her Majesty Queen Elizabeth…

QUEEN. *(offstage)* Have a care with my name, you'll wear it out. *(enters)* Oh, you are sick of self-love, Lord Chamberlain. The Queen of England does not attend exhibitions of public lewdness, so something is out of joint. Come here, Master Kent. Let me look at you.

> *(**VIOLA** comes forward and is about to curtsey, but stops and turns it into a sweeping bow.)*

Yes, the illusion is remarkable and your error, Tilney, easily forgiven. But I know something of a woman in a man's profession. Yes, by God, I do know about that. That is enough from you, Master Kent. If only Lord Wessex were here.

WEBSTER. He is, Ma'am. *(gets **WESSEX** from the trap)* Here he is. It's cold down there, isn't it, mate?

WESSEX. Unhand me, you stockfish. *(to **QUEEN**)* Your Majesty.

QUEEN. There was a wager, I remember…as to whether a play can show us the very truth and nature of love. I think you lost your wager today. *(to **WEBSTER**)* You are an eager boy. Did you like this play?

WEBSTER. I liked it when she stabbed herself.

QUEEN. And your name, young man?

WEBSTER. John Webster, Your Majesty.

QUEEN. You will go far.

WEBSTER. Cor…fanks!

QUEEN. *(fixes* WILL *with a beady eye)* Master Shakespeare. Next time you come to Greenwich, come as yourself and we will speak some more.

WESSEX. Your Majesty! How is this to end?

QUEEN. As stories must when love's denied – with tears and a journey. Those whom God has joined in marriage, not even I can put asunder. Master Kent – Lord Wessex, as I foretold, has lost his wife at the playhouse. Go make your farewell and send her out. It's time to settle accounts. How much was the wager?

WESSEX. Fifty shillings… *(off the* QUEEN*'s look)* Pounds.

QUEEN. Give it to Master Kent. He will see it rightfully home.

> *(*WESSEX *gives the purse to* VIOLA, *who turns and hands the money to* WILL.*)*

VIOLA. I believe this is rightfully yours, Master Shakespeare. I wish you a long and glorious career.

QUEEN. Master Shakespeare, something more cheerful next time…for Twelfth Night perhaps. Tragedy is all very well, sir, but remember, we very much like a dog.

> *[MUSIC NO. 43: "VIVAT QE1 EXIT"]*

> *(The* QUEEN *exits, followed by* WESSEX.*)*

TILNEY. I'll be revenged on the whole pack of you!

Scene Ten

[MUSIC NO. 44: "O MISTRESS MINE"]

(**VIOLA** *and* **WESSEX** *on board a ship. As the vessel leaves port, the* **COMPANY** *assemble and wave goodbye.*)

COMPANY. *(sung)*

O MISTRESS MINE, WHERE ARE YOU ROAMING?
O, STAY AND HEAR! YOUR TRUE LOVE'S COMING,
THAT CAN SING BOTH HIGH AND LOW.
TRIP NO FURTHER, PRETTY SWEETING;
JOURNEY'S END WITH LOVERS MEETING,
EVERY WISEMAN'S SON DOTH KNOW.
YOUTH'S A STUFF WILL NOT ENDURE.

Scene Eleven

(Will's room. **WILL** *is writing.* **MARLOWE** *appears.)*

MARLOWE. Not so bad after all, Will.

WILL. Angels and ministers of grace defend us. Are you a ghost?

MARLOWE. If I am not, I'll break my quill. I was right, you are quite good.

WILL. They said you were dead.

MARLOWE. Yes, they say that. Your health, Will.

WILL. And yours, Kit.

MARLOWE. What's next?

WILL. A new play. For Twelfth Night.

MARLOWE. Good title.

WILL. Really?

MARLOWE. And the comedy?

WILL. Comedy! What will my hero be but the saddest wretch in the kingdom, sick with love.

MARLOWE. Good start. Let him be…a duke.

WILL. Orsino.

MARLOWE. Good name. And your heroine?

WILL. Sold in marriage and halfway to America! And so my story begins at sea…a perilous voyage to an unknown land…a shipwreck—

MARLOWE. A shipwreck is good.

WILL. The wild waters roar and heave…the brave vessel is dashed all to pieces and all the hapless souls are drowned—

MARLOWE. A comedy?

WILL. —save one: a woman whose soul is greater than the ocean and her spirit stronger than the sea's embrace.

Not for her a watery end, but a new life beginning on a stranger shore, the province of the duke, Orsino.

MARLOWE. And then…

WILL. Fearful of her virtue she comes to him dressed as a boy.

MARLOWE. Thus unable to declare her love. Funny.

WILL. No, the comedy is with the clapped-out veterans and cross-gartered prigs who rule the household. Viola is the spirit of freedom, of true love trying against all bounds to be out.

MARLOWE. But how will it end?

*(**WILL** is back at his desk, writing furiously.)*

WILL. Happily.

MARLOWE. But how?

WILL. I don't know. It's a mystery.

The End

[MUSIC NO. 45: "CURTAIN CALL"]

[MUSIC NO. 46: "HOUSE OUT"]

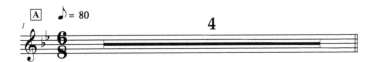

Bed Arrives

Pavane: What Is Love?

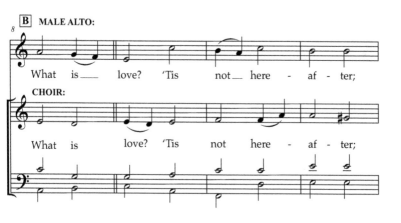

MALE ALTO:

What is love? 'Tis not here - af - ter;

CHOIR:

What is love? 'Tis not here - af - ter;

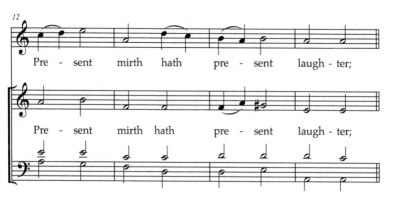

Pre - sent mirth hath pre - sent laugh - ter;

Pre - sent mirth hath pre - sent laugh - ter;

What's to — come is still - un - sure:

What's to come is still - un - sure:

Youth's a stuff will not en - dure.

Youth's — a — stuff will not en - dure.

D *(Under dialogue.)*
pp

What is — love? 'Tis not — here - af - ter;

pp

What is love? 'Tis not here - af - ter;

pp

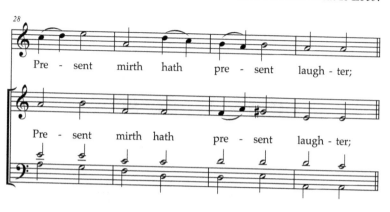

Pre - sent mirth hath pre - sent laugh - ter;

Pre - sent mirth hath pre - sent laugh - ter;

E

What's to ___ come is still - un - sure:

What's to come is still - un - sure:

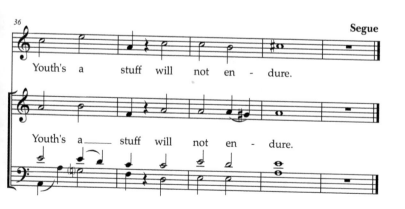

Segue

Youth's a stuff will not en - dure.

Youth's a ___ stuff will not en - dure.

Will Reads Viola's
Letter – Underscore

O   mis - tress   mine,   where   are   -   you   roam   -   ing?

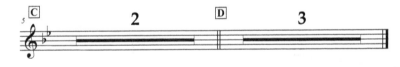

The Rowboat

22

O mis-tress mine, where   are you roam - ing?   Where are you

roam-ing?   O   mis - tress   mine? _____

O, stay and hear! your   true love's com - ing,   O, stay and

hear _____   O   mis - tress   mine. _____

Ooo

ALTO:

Ooo

Pavane to Bedroom

What's to ___ come is still un - sure:

What's to come is still un - sure:

Youth's a stuff will not en - dure.

Youth's _ a ___ stuff will not en - dure.

The Bedroom

25

Shall I Compare Thee

Vivat Regina – Entrance

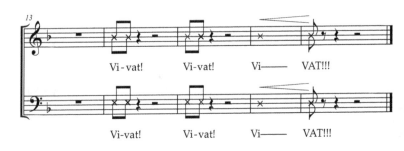

Marlowe's Death

MALE ALTO 1: E - ter - nal sum - mer

MALE ALTO 2: E - ter - nal sum - mer

TENOR: E - ter - nal sum - mer

BASS: But thy

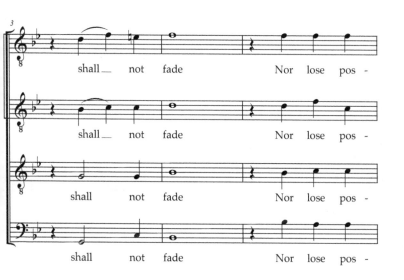

shall — not fade Nor lose pos -

shall — not fade Nor lose pos -

shall not fade Nor lose pos -

shall not fade Nor lose pos -

Death brag — thou wan - d'rest — in his

brag — thou wan - d'rest — in — his

Death brag thou wan - d'rest — in his

brag — thou wan - d'rest in — his

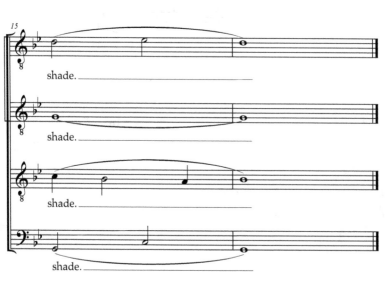

shade.—————————

shade.—————————

shade.—————————

shade.—————————

33

Wedding

♩ = 72

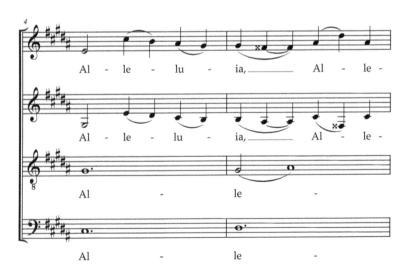

42

Juliet's Tomb

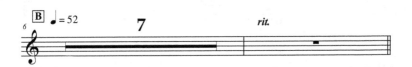

A tempo
MALE ALTO:

Ooo _____   Ooo _____

Ooo _____   Ooo _____

(Ooo) _____   Ooo _____

Ooo _____

Ooo _____

(Ooo) _____

Ooo _____

Ooo _____

44

O Mistress Mine

Jour - neys end in lov - ers meet - ing,

Ooh ooh, lov - ers meet - ing,

Ooh ooh, lov - ers meet - ing,

Ooh ooh, lov - ers meet - ing,

Ev' - ry wise man's son doth know, _____ doth

Ev' - ry wise man's son doth Ev' - ry wise man's son doth

Ev' - ry wise man's son doth know. _____

Ev' - ry wise man's son doth Ev' - ry wise man's son doth

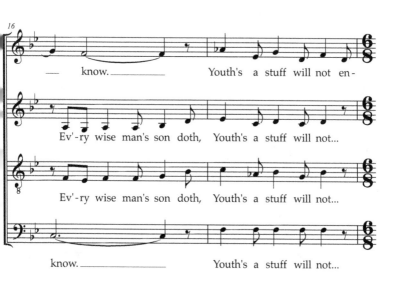

Ooh ooh, Ooh ooh,
Ooh ooh, Ooh ooh,
Ooh ooh, Ooh ooh,

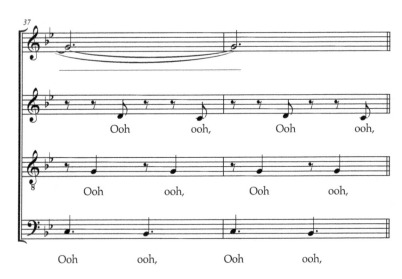

Ooh ooh, Ooh ooh,
Ooh ooh, Ooh ooh,
Ooh ooh, Ooh ooh,

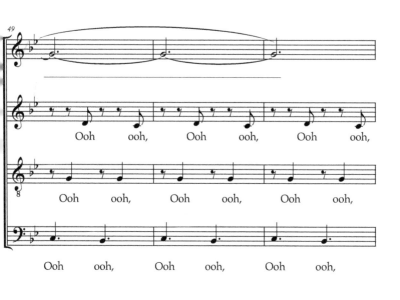

Ooh   ooh,   Ooh   ooh,   Ooh   ooh,

Ooh   ooh,   Ooh   ooh,   Ooh   ooh,

Ooh   ooh,   Ooh   ooh,   Ooh   ooh,

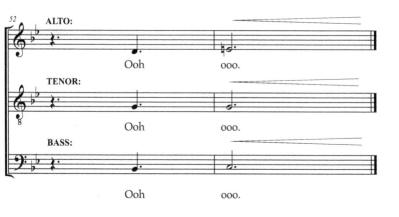

ALTO:

Ooh   ooo.

TENOR:

Ooh   ooo.

BASS:

Ooh   ooo.

CPSIA information can be obtained
at www.ICGtesting.com
Printed in the USA
BVHW072036261122
652661BV00008B/564

9 780573 705205